INDIANA SLAVE NARRATIVES

A Folk History of Slavery in Indiana
from Interviews with Former Slaves

* * *

Typewritten records prepared by
THE FEDERAL WRITERS' PROJECT
1936-1938

* * *

Published in cooperation witl
THE LIBRARY OF CONGRESS

D1088594

APPLEWOOD BOOKS
Bedford, Massachusetts

The LIBRARY
of CONGRESS

A portion of the proceeds from the sale
of this book is donated to the Library of
Congress, which holds the original Slave
Narratives in its collection.

Thank you for purchasing an Applewood book.
Applewood reprints America's lively classics
--books from the past that are still of
interest to modern readers. For a free copy
of our current catalog, write to:

Applewood Books
P.O. Box 365
Bedford, MA 01730

ISBN 1-55709-014-9

FOREWORD

More than 140 years have elapsed since the ratification of the Thirteenth Amendment to the U.S. Constitution declared slavery illegal in the United States, yet America is still wrestling with the legacy of slavery. One way to examine and understand the legacy of the 19th Century's "peculiar institution" in the 21st century is to read and listen to the stories of those who actually lived as slaves. It is through a close reading of these personal narratives that Americans can widen their understanding of the past, thus enriching the common memory we share.

The American Folklife Center at the Library of Congress is fortunate to hold a powerful and priceless sampling of sound recordings, manuscript interviews, and photographs of former slaves. The recordings of former slaves were made in the 1930s and early 1940s by folklorists John A. and Ruby T. Lomax, Alan Lomax, Zora Neale Hurston, Mary Elizabeth Barnicle, John Henry Faulk, Roscoe Lews, and others. These aural accounts provide the only existing sound of voices from the institution of slavery by individuals who had been held in bondage three generations earlier. These voices can be heard by visiting the web site http://memory.loc.gov/ammem/collections/voices/. Added to the Folklife Center collections, many of the narratives from manuscript sources, which you find in this volume, were collected under the auspices of the United States Works Progress Administration (WPA), and were known as the slave narrative collection. These transcripts are found in the Library of Congress Manuscript Division. Finally, in addition to the Folklife Center photographs, a treasure trove of Farm Security Administration (FSA) photographs (including those of many former slaves) reside in the Prints and Photographs Division here at the nation's library. Together, these primary source materials on audio tape, manuscript and photographic formats are a unique research collection for all who would wish to study and understand the emotions, nightmares, dreams, and determination of former slaves in the United States.

The slave narrative sound recordings, manuscript materials, and photographs are invaluable as windows through which we can observe and be touched by the experiences of slaves who lived in the mid-19th century. At the same time, these archival materials are the fruits of an extraordinary documentary effort of the 1930s. The federal government, as part of its response to the Great Depression, organized unprecedented national initiatives to document the lives, experiences, and cultural traditions of ordinary Americans. The slave narratives, as documents of the Federal Writers Project, established and delineated our modern concept of "oral history." Oral history, made possible by the advent of sound recording technology, was "invented" by folklorists, writers, and other cultural documentarians under the aegis of the Library of Congress and various WPA offices—especially the Federal Writers' project—during the 1930s. Oral history has subsequently become both a new tool for the discipline of history, and a new cultural pastime undertaken in homes, schools, and communities by Americans of all walks of life. The slave narratives you read in the pages that follow stand as our first national exploration of the idea of oral history, and the first time that ordinary Americans were made part of the historical record.

The American Folklife Center has expanded upon the WPA tradition by continuing to collect oral histories from ordinary Americans. Contemporary projects such as our Veterans History Project, StoryCorps Project, Voices of Civil Rights Project, as well as our work to capture the stories of Americans after September 11, 2001 and of the survivors of Hurricanes Katrina and Rita, are all adding to the Library of Congress holdings that will enrich the history books of the future. They are the oral histories of the 21st century.

Frederick Douglas once asked: can "the white and colored people of this country be blended into a common nationality, and enjoy together...under the same flag, the inestimable blessings of life, liberty, and the pursuit of happiness, as neighborly citizens of a common country? I believe they can." We hope that the words of the former slaves in these editions from Applewood Books will help Americans achieve Frederick Douglas's vision of America by enlarging our understanding of the legacy of slavery in all of our lives. At the same time, we in the American Folklife Center and the Library of Congress hope these books will help readers understand the importance of oral history in documenting American life and culture—giving a voice to all as we create our common history.

Peggy A. Bulger

Peggy Bulger
Director, The American Folklife Center
Library of Congress

A NOTE FROM THE PUBLISHER

Since 1976, Applewood Books has been republishing books from America's past. Our mission is to build a picture of America through its primary sources. The book you hold in your hand is a testament to that mission. Published in cooperation with the Library of Congress, this collection of slave narratives is reproduced exactly as writers in the Works Progress Administration's Federal Writers' Project (1936–1938) originally typed them.

As publishers, we thought about how to present these documents. Rather than making them more readable by resetting the type, we felt that there was more value in presenting the narratives in their original form. We believe that to fully understand any primary source, one must understand the period of time in which the source was written or recorded. Collected seventy years after the emancipation of American slaves, these narratives had been preserved by the Library of Congress, fortunately, as they were originally created. In 1941, the Library of Congress microfilmed the typewritten pages on which the narratives were originally recorded. In 2001, the Library of Congress digitized the microfilm and made the narratives available on their American Memory web site. From these pages we have reproduced the original documents, including both the marks of the writers of the time and the inconsistencies of the type. Some pages were missing or completely illegible, and we have used a simple typescript provided by the Library of Congress so that the page can be read. Although the font occasionally can make these narratives difficult to read, we believe that it is important not only to preserve the narratives of the slaves but also to preserve the documents themselves, thereby commemorating the groundbreaking effort that produced them. That way, also, we can give you, the reader, not only a collection of the life stories of ex-slaves, but also a glimpse into the time in which these stories were collected, the 1930s.

These are powerful stories by those who lived through slavery. No institution was more divisive in American history than slavery. From the very founding of America and to the present day, slavery has touched us all. We hope these real stories of real lives are preserved for generations of Americans to come.

INFORMANTS

130023

AN UNHAPPY EXPERIENCE.

This is written from an interview with each of the following: George W.
Arnold, Professor W. S. Best of the Lincoln High School and Samuel Bell,
all of Evansville, Indiana.

George W. Arnold was born April 7, 1861, in Bedford County, Tennessee.
He was the property of Oliver P. Arnold, who owned a large farm or plantation
in Bedford county. His mother was a native of Rome, Georgia, where she remained until twelve years of age, when she was sold at auction.

Oliver Arnold bought her, and he also purchased her three brothers and
one uncle. The four negroes were taken along with other slaves from Georgia
to Tennessee where they were put to work on the Arnold plantation.

On this plantation George W. Arnold was born and the child was allowed
to live in a cabin with his relatives and declares that he never heard one
of them speak an unkind word about Master Oliver Arnold or any member of his
family. "Happiness and contentment and a reasonable amount of food and clothes
seemed to be all we needed." said the now white-haired man.

Only a limited memory of Civil War days is retained by the old man but
the few events recalled are vividly described by him. "Mother, my young brother
my sister and I were walking along one day. I don't remember where we had
started but we passed under the fort at Wartrace.   A battle was in progress
and a large cannon was fired above us and we watched the huge ball sail throug
the air and saw the smoke of the cannon pass over our heads. We poor childrer
were almost scared to death but our mother held us close to her and tried to
comfort us. The next morning, after, we were safely at home, we were proud
we had seen that much of the great battle and our mother told us the war was
to give us freedom."

"Did your family rejoice when they were set free? was the natural question

Ex-Slave Stories
District No.5
Vanderburgh County
Lauana Creel .

‡2.   2

AN UNHAPPY EXPERIENCE.

TC ask Uncle George.

"I cannot say that they were happy, as it broke up a lot of real friend-ships and scattered many families. Mother had a great many pretty quilts and a lot of bedding. After the negroes were set free, Mars. Arnold told us we could all go and make ourselves homes, so we started out, each of the grown persons/ loaded with great bundles of bedding, clothing and personal belong-ings. We walked all the way to Wartrace to try to find a home and some way to make a living."

George W. Arnold remembers seeing many soldiers going to the pike road on their way to Murfreesboro. "Long lines of tired men passed through Guy's Gap on their way to Murfreesboro." said he, "Older people said that they were sent out to pick up the dead from the battle fields after the bloody battle of Stone's river that had lately been fought at Murfreesboro. They took their comrads to bury them at the Union Cemetery near the town of Mur-freesboro."

"Wartrace was a very nice place to make our home. It was located on the Nashville and Chattanooga and St. Louis railroad, just fifty-one miles from Nashville not many miles from our old home."   "Mother found work and we got along very well but as soon as we children were old enough to work, she went back to her old home in Georgia where a few years later she died. I believe she lived to be seventy-five or seventy six years of age, but I never saw her after she went back to Georgia."

"My first work was done on a farm (there are many fine farms in Tennessee) and although farm labor was not very profitable we were always fed wherever we worked and got some wages.   Then I got a job on the railroad. "Our car was side tracked at a place called Silver Springs." said Uncle George, "and right at that place came trouble that took the happiness out of my life forever.

AN UNHAPPY EXPERIENCE.

Here the story teller paused to collect his thoughts and conquer the nervous
twitching of his lips. "It was like this: Three of us boys worked together.
We were like three brothers, always sharing our fortunes with each other. We
should never have done it, but we had made a habit of sending to Nashville
after each payday and having a keg of Holland rum sent in by freight. This
liquor was handed out among our friends and sometimes we drank too much and
were unfit for work for a day or two. Our boss was a big strong Irishman,
red haired and friendly. He always got drunk with us and all would become
sober enough to soon return to our tasks.

"The time I'm telling you about, we had all been invited to a candy pull-
ing in town and could hardly wait till time to go, as all the young people of
the valley would be there to pull candy, talk, play games and eat the goodies
served to us. The accursed keg of Holland rum had been brought in that morning and my chum John Sims had been drinking too much. About that time our Boss
came up and said, "John, it is time for you to get the supper ready!' John
was our cook and our meals were served on the caboose where we lived wherever
we were side tracked.

All the time Johny was preparing the food he was drinking the rum. When
we went in he had many drinks inside of him and a quart bottle filled to take
to the candy pull. 'Hurry up boys and let's finish up and go' he said impati-
ently. 'Don't take him' said the other boy, 'Dont you see he is drunk?"
So I put my arms about his shoulders and tried to tell him he had better sleep
a while before we started. The poor boy was a breed. His mother was almost
white and his father was a thorough bred Indian and the son had a most aggra-
vating temper. He made me no answer but running his hand into his pocket,
he drew out his knife and with one thrust, cut a deep gash in my neck. A
terrible fight followed. I remember being knocked over and my head striking

AN UNHAPPY EXPERIENCE.

something. I reached out my hand and discovered it was the ax. With this awful weapon I struck my friend, my more than brother. The thud of the ax brought me to my senses as our blood mingled. We were both almost mortally wounded. The boss came in and tried to do something for our relief but John said, "Oh, George? what an awful thing we have done? We have never said a cross word to each other and now, look at us both ."

"I watched poor John walk away, darkness was falling but early in the morning my boss and I followed a trail of blood down by the side of the tracks. From there he had turned into the woods. We could follow him no further. We went to all the nearby towns and villages but we found no person who had ever seen him. We supposed he had died in the woods and watched for the buzzards, thinking they would lead us to his body but he was never seen again.

For two years I never sat down to look inside a book nor to eat my food that John Sims was not beside me. He haunted my pillow and went beside me night and day. His blood was on my hands, his presence haunted me beyond endurance. What could I do? How could I escape this awful presence? An old friend told me to put water between myself and the place where the awful scene occurred. So, I quit working on the railroad and started working on the river. People believed at that time that the ghost of a person you had wronged would not cross water to haunt you. "

Life on the river was diverting. Things were constantly happening and George Arnold put aside some of his unhappiness by engaging in river activities.

"My first job on the river was as a roust-about on the Bolliver H Cook a stern wheel packet which carried freight and passengers from Nashville,Tennessee to Evansville, Indiana. I worked a round trip on her then went from

AN UNHAPPY EXPERIENCE.

Nashville to Cairo, Illinois on the B. S. Rhea. I soon decided to go to
Cairo and take a place on the Eldarado, a St. Louis and Cincinnati packet
which crused from Cairo to Cincinnati.   On that boat I worked as a roust-
about for nearly three years."

        "What did the roust-about have to do?" asked a neighbor lad who had come
into the room.   "The roust-about is no better than the mate that rules him.
If the mate is kindly disposed the roust-about has an easy enough life. The
negroes had only a few years of freedom and resented cruelty. If the mate
became too mean, a regular fight would follow and perhaps several roust-abouts
would be hurt before it was finished."

        Uncle George said that food was always plentiful on the boats. Passengers
and freight were crowded together on the decks.   At night there would be sing-
ing and dancing and fiddle music.   We roust-abouts would get together and
shoot craps, dance or play cards until the call came to shuffle freight, then
we would all get busy and the mate's voice givving orders could be heard for
a long distance.

        "Inspite of these few pleasures, the life of a roust-about is the life of
a dog.   I do not recall any unkindnesses of slavery days. I was too young
to realize what it was all about, but it could never have equalled the cruelty shown the laborer on the river boats by cruel mates and overseers."

        Another superstition advanced itself in the story of a boat, told by Uncle
George Arnold. The story follows: "When I was a roust-about on the Gold
Dust We were sailing out from New Orleans and as soon as we got well out on
the broad stream the rats commenced jumping over board. 'See these rats' said
an old river man, 'This boat will never make a return trip!!

        "At every port some of our crew left the boat but the mate and the captain
said they were all fools and begged us to stay. So a few of us stayed to do

An Unhappy Experience.

the necessary work but the rats kept leaving as fast as they could.

"When the boat was nearing Hickman, Kentucky, we smelled fire, and by the time we were in the harpor passengers were being held to keep them from jumping over board.   Then the Captain told us boys to jump into the water and save ourselves. Two of us launched a bale of cotton over-board and jumped onto it. As we paddled away we had to often go under to put out the fires as our clothing would blaze up under the flying brands that fell upon our bodies

"The burning boat was docked at Hickman. The passengers were put ashore but none of the freight was saved, and from a nearby willow thicket my matey and I watched the Gold Dust burn to the water's edge.

"Always heed the warnings of nature," said Uncle George, "If you see rats leaving a ship or a house prepare for a fire."

George W. Arnold said that Evansville was quite a nice place and a steamboat port even in the early days of his boating experiences and he decided to make his home here. He located in the town in 1880. "The Court House was located at Third and Main streets. Street cars were mule drawn and people thought it great fun to ride them." He recalls the first shovel full of dirt being lifted when the new Courthouse was being erected, and when it was finished two white men who finishing the slate roof, fell to their death in the Court House yard.

George W. Arnold procured a job as porter in a wholesale feed store on May 10, 1880. John Hubbard and Company did business at the place, at this place he worked thirty seven years. F.W.Griese, former mayor of Evansville has often befriended the negro man and is ready to speak a kindly word in his praise. But the face of John Sims still presents itself when George Arnold is alone. "Never do anything to hurt any other person," says he, "The hurt always comes back to you."

AN UNHAPPY EXPERIENCE.

George Arnold was married to an Evansville Woman, but two years ago he became a widower when death claimed his mate.   He is now lonely, but were it not for a keg of Holland gin his old age would be spent in peace and happiness.   "Beware of strong drink," said Uncle George, "It causes trouble.

REMINISCENCES OF TWO EX-SLAVES.

References:

A. Thomas Ash, ex-slave, Mitchell, Ind.

B. Mrs. Mary Crane, ex-slave, Warren St., Mitchell, Ind.

I have no way of knowing exactly how old I am, as the old Bible containing a record of my birth was destroyed by fire, many years ago, but I believe I am about eighty-one years old. If so, I must have been born sometime during the year, 1856, four years before the outbreak of the War Between The States. My mother was a slave on the plantation, or farm of Charles Ash, in Anderson county, Kentucky, and it was there that I grew up.

I remember playing with Ol' Massa's (as he was called) boys, Charley, Jim and Bill. I also have an unpleasant memory of having seen other slaves on the place, tied up to the whipping post and flogged for disobeying some order although I have no recollection of ever having been whipped myself as I was only a boy. I can also remember how the grown-up negroes on the place left to join the Union Army as soon as they learned of Lincoln's proclamation making them free men.   (A)

Ed. Note --Mr. Ash was sick when interviewed and was not able to do much talking. He had no picture of himself but agreed to pose for one later on.

I was born on the farm of Wattie Williams, in 1855 and am eighty-two years old. I came to Mitchell, Indiana, about fifty years ago with my husband, who is now dead and four children and have lived here ever since. I was only a girl, about five or six years old when the Civil War broke out but I can remember very well, happenings of that time.

My mother was owned by Wattie Williams, who had a large farm, located in Larue county, Kentucky. My father wasa slave on the farm of a Mr. Duret, nearby.

In those days, slave owners, whenever one of their daughters would get married, would give her and her husband a slave as a wedding present, usually allowing the girl to pick the one she wished to accompany her to her new home. When Mr. Duret's eldest daughter married Zeke Samples, she choose my father to accompany them to their home.

Zeke Samples proved to be a man who loved his toddies far better than his bride and before long he was "broke". Everything he had or owned, including my father, was to be sold at auction to pay off his debts.

In those days, there were men who made a business of buying up negroes at auction sales and shipping them down to New Orleans to be sold to owners of cotton and sugar cane plantations, just as men today, buy and ship cattle. These men were called "Nigger-traders" and they would ship whole boat loads at a time, buying them up, two or three here, two or three there, and holding them in a jail until they had a boat load. This practice gave rise to the expression, "sold down the river."

My father was to be sold at auction, along with all of the rest of Zeke Samples' property. Bob Cowherd, a neighbor of Matt Duret's owned my grandfather, and the old man, my grandfather, begged Col. Bob to buy my father from Zeke Samples to keep him from being "sold down the river." Col. Bob offered what he thought was a fair price for my father and a "nigger-trader" raised his bid "25. Col. said he couldn't afford to pay that much and father was about to be sold to the "nigger-trader" when his father told Col. Bob that he had $25 saved up and that if he would buy my father from Samples and keep the "nigger-trader" from gettin/him he would give him the money. Col. Bob Cowherd took my grandfather's $25 and offered to meet the traders offer and so my father was sold to him.

The negroes in and around where I was raised were not treated badly, as a rule, by their masters. There was one slave owner, a Mr. Heady, who lived nearby, who treated his slave worse than any of the other owners but l never heard of anything so awfully bad, happening to his "niggers". He had one boy who used to come over to our place and I can remember hearing Massa Williams call to my grandmother, to cook "Christine, give "Heady's Doc something to eat. He looks hungry." Massa Williams always said "Heady's Doc" when speaking of him or any other slave, saying to call him, for instance, Doc Heady would sound as if he were Mr. Heady's own son and he said that wouldn't sound right.

When President Lincoln issued his proclamation, freeing the negroes, I remember that my father and most all of the other younger slave men left the farms to join the Union army. We had hard times then for awhile and had lots of work to do. I don't remember just when I xxx first regarded myself as "free" as many of the negroes didn't understand just what it was all about.   (B)
Ed. Note: Mrs. Crane will also pose for a picture.

Submitted by:
William Webb Tuttle -
District No. 2
Muncie, Indiana

SLAVES IN DELAWARE COUNTY
ROSA BARBER

Reference: Rosa Barber, residing at 812 South Jefferson, .
             Muncie, Indiana.

Rosa Barber was born in slavery on the Fox Ellison plantation
at North Carden, In North Carolina, in the year 1861. She was four ?
years old when freed, but had not reached the age to be of value
as a slave. Her memory is confined to that short childhood there
and her experiences of those days and immediately after the Civil
War must be taken from stories related to her by her parents in
after years, and these are dimly retained.

Her maiden name was Rosa Fox Ellison, taken as was the custom,
from the slave-holder who held her as a chattel. Her parents took
her away from the plantation when they were freed and lived in
different localities, supported by the father who was now paid
American wages. Her parents died while she was quite young and she
married Fox Ellison, an ex-slave of the Fox Ellison plantation. His
name was taken from the same master as was hers. She and her husband
lived together forty-three years, until his death. Nine children
were born to them of which only one survives. After this ex-slave
husband died Rosa Ellison married a second time, but this second
husband died some years ago and she now remains a widow at the age
of seventy-six years. She recalls that the master of the Fox Ellison
plantation was spoken of as practicing no extreme discipline on his
slaves. Slaves, as a prevailing business policy of the holder, were
not allowed to look into a book, or any printed matter, and Rosa
had no pictures or printed charts given her. She had to play with

her rag dolls, or a ball of yarn, if there happened to be enought
of old string to make one. Any toy or plaything was allowed that
did not point toward book-knowledge. Nursery rhymes and folk-lore
stories were censured severly and had to be confined to events that
conveyed no uplift, culture or propaganda, or that conveyed no
knowledge, directly or indirectly. Especially did they bar the
mental polishing of the three R's.   They could not prevent the
vocalizing of music in the fields and the slaves found consolation
there in pouring out their souls in unison with the songs of the
birds.

Federal Writers' Project
of the W. P. A.
District #6
Marion County
File #64-A

Page #1
Topic #240
Anna Pritchett

Folklore

References

 (A) Mr. Mittie Blakeley -Ex-slave-

   2055 Columbia Avenue, Indianapolis, Indiana.

 (B) Anna Pritchett -Federal Writer-

   1200 Kentucky Avenue, Indianapolis, Indiana.

Mrs. Blakeley was born, in Oxford, Missouri, in 1858. (A)

Her mother died when Mittie was a baby, and she was taken into the "big house" and brought up with the white children. She was always treated very kindly. (A)

Her duties were the light chores, which had to be well done, or she was chided, the same as the white children would have been. (A)

Every evening the children had to collect the eggs. The child, who brought in the most eggs, would get a ginger cake. Mittie most always got the cake. (A)

Her older brothers and sisters were treated very rough, whipped often and hard. She said she hated to think, much less talk about their awful treatment. (A)

When she was old enough, she would have to spin the wool for her mistress, who wove the cloth to make the family clothes. (A)

She also learned to knit, and after supper would knit until bedtime. (A)

She remembers once an old woman slave had displeased her master about something. He had a pit dug, and boards placed over the hole. The woman was made to lie on the boards, face down, and she was beaten until the blood gushed from her body; she was left there and bled to death. (A)

She also remembers how the slaves would go to some cabin at night for their dances; if one went without a pass, which often they did, they would be beaten severely. (A)

The slaves could hear the overseers, riding toward the cabin. Those, who had come without a pass, would take the boards up from the floor, get under the cabin floor, and stay there until the overseers had gone. (A)

Mrs. Blakeley is very serious and said she felt so sorry for those, who were treated so much worse than any human would treat a beast. (B)

She lives in a very comfortable clean house, and said she was doing "very well." (B)

Submitted January 24, 1938
Indianapolis, Indiana

By: ANNA PRITCHETT
      Field Writer

SLAVES IN MADISON COUNTY
CARL BOONE

Reference: Personal interview with Carl Boone, Anderson, Indiana

This is a story of slavery, told by Carl Boone about his father, his mother and himself. Carl is the last of eighteen children born to Mrs. Stephen Boone, in Marion County, Kentucky, Sept. 15, 1850. He now resides with his children at 801 West 13th Street, Anderson, Madison County, Indiana. At the ripe old age of eighty-seven, he still has a keen memory and is able to do a hard day's work.

Carl Boone was born a free man, fifteen years before the close of the Civil War, his father having gained his freedom from slavery in 1829. He is a religious man, having missed church service only twice in twenty years. He was treated well during the time of slavery in the southland, but remembers well, the wrongs done to slaves on neighboring plantations, and in this story he relates some of the horrors which happened at that time!

Like his father, he is also the father of eighteen children, sixteen of whom are still living. He is grandfather of thirty-seven and great grandfather of one child. His father was born in the slave state of Maryland, in 1800, and died in 1897. His mother was born in Marion County, Kentucky, in 1802, and died in 1917, at the age of one hundred and fifteen years.

This story, word by word, is related by Carl Boone as follows: "My name is Carl Boone, son of Stephen and Rachel Boone, born in Marion County, Kentucky, in 1850. I am father of eighteen children sixteen are still living and I am grandfather of thirty-seven and

great grandfather of one child. I came with my wife, now deceased,
to Indiana, in 1891, and now reside at 801 West 13th street in
Anderson, Indiana. I was born a free man, fifteen years before the
close of the Civil War. All the colored folk on plantations and
farms around our plantation were slaves and most of them were terribly
mistreated by their masters.

After coming to Indiana, I farmed for a few years, then moved
to Anderson. I became connected with the Colored Catholic Church
and have tried to live a Christian life. I have only missed church
service twice in twenty years. I lost my dear wife thirteen years
ago and I now live with my son.

My father, Stephen Boone, was born in Marylnad, in 1800. He
was bought by a nigger buyer while a boy and was sold to Miley Boone
in Marion County, Kentucky. Father was what they used to call"a
picked slave," was a good worker and was never mistreated by his
master. He married my mother in 1825, and they had eighteen children.
Master Miley Boone gave father and mother their freedom in 1829,
and gave them forty acres of land to tend as their own. He paid
father for all the owrk he did for him after that, and was always
very kind to them.

My mother was born in slavery, in Marion County, Kentucky, in
1802. She was treated very mean until she married my father in 1825.
With him she gained her freedom in 1829. I was the last born of her
eighteen children. She wasa good woman and joined church after
coming to Indiana and died in 1917, living to be one hundred and
fifteen years old.

I have heard my mother tell of a girl slave who worked in the
kitchen of my mother's master. The girl was told to cook twelve eggs

for breakfast. When the eggs were served, it was discovered there were eleven eggs on the table and after being questioned, she admitted that she had eaten one. For this, she was beaten mercilessly, which was a common sight on that plantation.

The most terrible treatment of any slave, is told by my father in a story of a slave on a neighboring plantation, owned by Daniel Thompson. "After committing a small wrong, Master Thompson became angry, tied his slave to a whipping post and beat him terribly. Mrs. Thompson begged him to quit whipping, saying, 'you might kill him,' and the master replied that he aimed to kill him. He then tied the slave behind a horse and dragged him over a fifty acre field until the slave was dead. As a punishment for this terrible deed, master Thompson was compelled to witness the execution of his own son, one year later. The story is as follows:

A neighbor to Mr. Thompson, a slave owner by name of Kay Van-Cleve, had been having some trouble with one of his young male slaves, and had promised the slave a whipping. The slave was a powerful man and Mr. Van Cleve was afraid to undertake the job of whipping him alone. He called for help from his neighbors, Daniel Thompson and his son Donald. The slave, while the Thompsons were coming, concealed himself in a horse-stall in the barn and hid a large knife in the manger.

After the arrival of the Thompsons, they and Mr. Van Cleve entered the stall in the barn. Together, the three white men made a grab for the slave, when the slave suddenly made a lunge at the elder Mr. Thompson with the knife, but missed him and stabbed Donald Thompson,

The slave was overpowered and tied, but too late, young Donald was dead.

Slaves in Madison County
Carl Boone

The slave was tried for murder and sentenced to be hanged.
At the time of the hanging, the first and second ropes used broke
when the trap was sprung. For a while the executioner considered f
freeing the slave because of his second failure to hang him, but
the law said, "He shall hang by the neck until dead," and the third
attempt was successful. "

Federal Writers' Project
   of the W. P. A.
   District #6
   Marion County
   File #57-A

                                 Page #1
                                 Topic #240
                                 Anna Pritchett

Folklore

Reference:

    (A) Mrs. Julia Bowman -Ex-slave, 1210 North West street,
         Indianapolis, Indiana.

    (B) Anna Pritchett, Federal Writer, 1200 Kentucky avenue,
         Indianapolis, Indiana.

Mrs. Bowman was born in Woodford County, Kentucky in 1859. (A)

Her master, Joel W. Twyman was kind and generous to all of his slaves, and he had many of them. (A)

The Twyman slaves were always spoken of, as the Twyman "Kinfolks." (A)

All slaves worked hard on the large farm, as every kind of vegetation was raised. They were given some of everything that grew on the farm, therefore there was no stealing to get food. (A)

The master had his own slaves, and the mistress had her own slaves, and all were treated very kindly. (A)

Mrs. Bowman was taken into the Twyman "big house," at the age of six, to help the mistress in any way she could. She stayed in the house until slavery was abolished. (A)

After freedom, the old master was taken very sick and some of the former slaves were sent for, as he wanted some of his "Kinfolks" around him when he died. (A)

Mrs. Bowman was given the Twyman family bible where her birth is recorded with the rest of the Twyman family. She shows it with pride. (B)

Mrs. Bowman said she never knew want in slave times, as she has known it in these times of depression. (B)

Submitted January 10, 1938
Indianapolis, Indiana

By: ANNA PRITCHETT
    Field Writer

ANGIE BOYCE
born in slavery, Mar. 14, 1861 on the
Breeding Plantation, Adair Co. Ky.

Mrs. Angie Boyce here makes mention of facts as outlined to her by her mother, Mrs. Margaret King, deceased.

Mrs. Angie Boyce was born in slavery, Mar. 14, 1861, on the Breeding Plantation, Adair County, Kentucky. Her parents were Henry and Margaret King who belonged to James Breeding, a Methodist minister who was kind to all his slaves and no remembrance of his having ever struck one of them.

It is said that the slaves were in constant dread of the Rebel soldiers and when they would hear of their coming they would hide the baby "Angie" and cover her over with leaves.

The mother of Angie was married twice; the name of her first ### husband was Stines and that of her second husband was Henry King. It was Henry King who bought his and his wife's freedom. He sent his wife and baby Angie to Indiana, but upon their arrival they were arrested and returned to Kentucky. They were placed in the Louisville jail and lodged in the same cell with large brutal and drunken Irish woman. The jail was so infested with bugs and fleas that the baby Angie cryed all night. The white woman crazed with drink became enraged at the cries of the child and threatened to "bash its brains out against the wall if it did not stop crying". The mother, Mrs. King was forced to stay awake all night to keep the white woman from carrying out her threat.

The next morning the Negro mother was tried in court and when she produced her free papers she was asked why she did not show these papers to the arresting officers. She replied that she was afraid that they would steal them from her. She was exonerated from all charges and sent back to Indiana with her baby.

Mrs. Angie Boyce now resides at 498 W. Madison St., Franklin, Ind.

Life Story of Ex-Slave

(Mrs. Edna Boysaw)

Personal interview by the writer.

Mrs. Boysaw has been a citizen of this community about sixty-five years. She resides on a small farm, two miles east of Brazil on what is known as the Pinkley Street Road. This has been her home for the past forty years. Her youngest son and the son of one of her daughters lives with her. She is still very active, doing her housework and other chores about the farm. She is very intelligent and according to statements made by other citizens has always been a respected citizen in the community, as also has her entire family. She is the mother of twelve children. Mrs. Boysaw has always been an active church worker, spending much time in missionary work for the colored people. Her work was so outstanding that she has been often called upon to speak, not only in the colored churches, but also in white churches, where she was always well received. Many of the most prominent people of the community number Mrs. Boysaw as one of their friends and her home is visited almost daily by citizens in all walks of life. Her many acts of kindness towards her neighbors and friends have endeared her to the people of Brazil, and because of her long residence in the community, she is looked upon as one of the pioneers.

Mrs. Boysaw's husband has been dead for thirty-five years. Her children are located in various cities throughout the country. She has a daughter who is a talented singer, and has appeared on programs with her daughter in many churches. She is not certain about her age, but according to her memory of events, she is about eighty-seven.

Her story as told to the writer follows:

"When the Civil War ended, I was living near Richmond, Virginia. I am not sure just how old I was, but I was a big, flat-footed woman, and had worked as a slave on a plantation. My master was a good one, but many of them were not. In a way, we were happy and contented, working from sun up to sun down. But when Lincoln freed us, we rejoiced, yet we knew we had to seek employment now and make our own way. Wages were low. You worked from morning until night for a dollar, but we did not complain. About 1870 a Mr. Masten, who was a coal operator, came to Richmond seeking laborers for his mines in Clay County. He told us that men could make four to five dollars a day working in the mines, going to work at seven and quitting at 3:30 each day. That sounded like a Paradise to our men folks. Big money and you could get rich in little time. But he did not tell all, because he wanted the men folk to come with him to Indiana. Three or four hundred came with Mr. Masten. They were brought in box cars. Mr. Masten paid their transportation, but was to keep it out of their wages. My husband was in that bunch, and the women folk stayed behind until their men could earn enough for their transportation to Indiana."

"When they arrived about four miles east of Brazil, or what was known as Harmony, the train was stopped and a crowd of white miners ordered them not to come any nearer Brazil. Then the trouble began. Our men did not know of the labor trouble, as they were not told of that part. Here they were fifteen hundred miles from home, no money. It was terrible. Many walked back to Virginia. Some went on foot to Illinois. Mr. Masten took some of them South of Brazil about three miles, where he had a number of company houses, and they tried to work in his mine there. But many were shot at from the bushes and killed. Guards were placed about the mine by the owner, but still there was trouble all the time. The men did not make what Mr. Masten told them they could make, yet they had to stay for they had no place to go. After about six months, my husband who had been working in that mine, fell into the shaft and was injured. He was unable to work

for over a year. I came with my two children to take care of him. We had
only a little furniture, slept in what was called box beds. I walked to
Brazil each morning and worked at whatever I could get to do. Often did
three washings a day and then walked home each evening, a distance of two
miles, and got a dollar a day.

"Many of the white folks I worked for were well to do and often I would
ask the Mistress for small amounts of food which they would throw out if
left over from a meal. They did not know what a hard time we were having,
but they told me to take home any of such food that I cared to. I was sure
glad to get it, for it helped to feed our family. Often the white folks
would give me other articles which I appreciated. I managed in this way
to get the children enough to eat and later when my husband was able to work,
we got along very well, and were thankful. After the strike was settled, things
were better. My husband was not afraid to go out after dark. But the coal
operators did not treat the colored folks very good. We had to trade at the
Company store and often pay a big price for it. But I worked hard and am
still alive today, while all the others are gone, who lived around here about
that time. There has sure been a change in the country. The country was
almost a wilderness, and where my home is today, there were very few roads,
just what we called a pig path through the woods. We used lots of corn meal,
cooked beans and raised all the food we could during them days. But we had
many white friends and sure was thankful for them. Here I am, and still
thankful for the many friends I have."

Federal Writers' Project
    of the W. P. A.
    District #6
    Marion County
    File #53-A

Page #1
Topic #240
Anna Pritchett

Folklore

References

    (A) Mrs. Callie Bracey -daughter- 414 Blake street.

    (B) Anna Pritchett -Federal Writers'Project- 1200 Kentucky
        avenue, Indianapolis, Indiana.

      Mrs. Callie Bracey's mother, Louise Terrell, was bought,
when a child, by Andy Ramblet, a farmer, near Jackson, Miss. She had
to work very hard in the fields from early morning until as late in the
evening, as they could possibly see. (A)

      No matter how hard she had worked all day after coming in
from the field, she would have to cook for the next day, packing the
lunch buckets for the field hands. It made no difference how tired
she was, when the horn was blown at 4 a.m., she had to go into the field
for another day of hard work. (A)

      The women had to split rails all day long, just like the men.
Once she got so cold, her feet seemed to be frozen; when they warmed a
little, they had swollen so, she could not wear her shoes. She had to

wrap her feet in burlap, so she would be able to go into the field
the next day. (A)

The Ramblets were known for their good butter. They always
had more than they could use. The master wanted the slaves to have
some, but the mistress wanted to sell it, she did not believe in giving
good butter to slaves and always let it get strong before she would
let them have any. (A)

No slaves from neighboring farms were allowed on the Ramblet
farm, they would get whipped off as Mr. Ramblet didnot want anyone
to put ideas in his slave's heads. (A)

On special occasions, the older slaves were allowed to go to
the church of their master, they had to sit in the back of the church,
and take no part in the service. (A)

Louise was given two dresses a year; her old dress from last
year, she wore as an underskirt. She never had a hat, always wore a rag
tied over her head. (A)

Mrs. Bracey is a widow and has a grandchild living with her.
She feels she is doing very well, her parents had so little, and she does
own her own home.

Submitted December 10, 1937
Indianapolis, Indiana

By: ANNA PRITCHETT
        Field Writer

A Slave, Ambassador and City Doctor.

This paper was prepared after several interviews had been obtained
with the subject of this sketch.

Dr. George Washingtin Buckner, tall, lean, whitehaired, genial
and alert, answered the call of his door bell. Although anxious to
oblige the writer and willing to grant an interview, the life of a
city doctor is filled with anxious solicitation for others and he is
always expecting a summons to the bedside of a patient or a professional interview has been slated.

Dr. Buckner is no exception and our interviews were often disturbed by the jingle of the door bell or a telephone call.

Dr. Buckner's conversation lead in ever widening circles, away from
the topic under discussion when the events of his own life were discussed, but he is a fluent speaker and a student of psychology. Psychology
as that philosophy relates to the mental and bodily tendencies of the
African race has long since become one of the major subjects with which
this unusual man struggles.   "Why is the negro?" is one of his deep-
est concerns.

Dr. Buckner's first recollections center within a slave cabin in
Kentucky. The cabin was the home of his step-father, his invalid mother
and several children. The cabin was of the crudest construction, its
only windows being merely holes in the cabin wall with crude bark shut-
ters arranged to keep out snow and rain.   The furnishings of this
home consisted of a wood bedstead upon which a rough straw bed and
patchwork wuilts provided meager comforts for the invalid mother. A
straw bed that could be pushed under the bed-stead through the day was
pulled into the middle of the cabin at night and the wearied children
were put to bed by the impatient step-father.

The parents were slaves and served a master not wealthy enough to

A Slave, Ambassador, and City Doctor.

provide adaquately for their comforts.   The mother had become invalid-
ate through the task of bearing children each year and being deprived
of medical and surgical attention.

The master, Mr. Buckner, along with several of his relatives had
purchased a large tract of land in Green County, Kentucky and by a
custom or tradition as Dr. Buckner remembers; land owners that owned
no slaves were considered "Po' White Trash" and were scarcely recognized
as citizens within the stateof Kentucky.

Another tradition prevailed, that slave children should be presented to the master's young sons and daughters and become their special
property even in childhood. Adherring to that tradition the child,
George Washington Buckner became the slave of young "Mars" Dickie Buckner, and although the two children were nearly the same age the little
mulatto boy was obedient to the wishes of the little master.   Indeed,
the slave child cared for the Caucassian boy's clothing, polished his
boots, put away his toys and was his playmate and companion as well as
his slave.

Sickness and suffering and even death visits alike the just and the
unjust, and the loving sympathetic slave boy witnessed the suffering and
death of his little white friend.   Then grief took possession of the
little slave, he could not bear the sight of little Dick's toys nor
books not clothing. He recalls one harrowing experience after the death
of little Dick Buckner. George's grandmother was a housekeeper and
kitchen maid for the white family. She was in the kitchen one late afternoon preparing the evening meal. The master had taken his family
for a visit in the neighborhood and the mulatto child sat on the veranda
and recalled pleasanter days. A sudden desire seized him to look into
the bed room where little Mars Dickie had lain in the bed. The evening

Ex-Slave Stories
District #5
Vanderburgh County
Lauana Creel
:3. 29
A Slave, Ambassador and City Doctor.

shaddows had fallen, exagerated by the influence of trees/ and vines,
and when he placed his pale face near the window pane he thought it was
the face of little Dickie looking out at him.   His nerves gave away
and he ran around the house screaming to his grandmother that he had
seen Dickie's ghost.   The old colored woman was sympathetic, dried his
tears, then with tears coursing down her own cheeks she went about her
duties.   George firmly believed he had seen a ghost and never really
convinced himself against the idea until he had reached the years of
manhood.   He remembers how the story reached the ears of the other slaves
and they were terrorized at the suggestion of a ghost being in the master's home.   "That is the way superstitions always started" said the Doctor, "Some nervous persons received a wrong impression and there were
always others ready to embrace the error."   ..

Dr. Buckner remembers that when a young daughter of his master
married, his sister was given to her for a bridal gift and went away
from her own mother to live in the young mistress' new home.   "It always
filled us with sorrow when we were separated either by circumstances of
marriage or death.   Although we were not properly housed, properly nour-
ished nor properly clothed we loved each other and loved our cabin homes
and were unhappy when compelled to part."

"There are many beautiful spots near the Green River and our home
was situated near Greensburgh, the county seat of Dreen County.   The
area occupied by Mr. Buckner and his relatives is located near the river
and the meanderings of the stream almost formed a peninsula covered with
rich soil.   Buckner's hill relieved the landscape and clear springs bub-
led through crevices affording much water for household use and near those
springs white and negro children met to enjoy themselves.

"Forty years after I left Greensburg I went back to visit the springs
and try to meet my old friends./ The friends had passed away, only a few

Ex*Slave Stories
District #5
Vanderburgh County
Lauana Creel   A Slave, Ambassador and City Doctor.

4.   38

merchants and salespeople remembered my ancestors."

A story told by Dr. Buckner relates an evening at the beginning of the Civil War. "I had heard my parents talk of the war but it did not seem real to me until one night when mother came to the pallet where we slept and called to us to "Get up and tell our uncles good-bye." Then four startled little children arose. Mother was standing in the room with a candle or a sort of torch made from grease drippings and old pieces of cloth, (these rude candles were in common use and afforded but poor light) and there stood her four brothers, Jacob, John, Bill, and Isaac all with the light of adventure shinhing upon their mulatto countenances. They were starting away to fight for their liberties and we were greatly impressed."

Dr. Buckner stated that officials thought Jacob entirely too aged to enter the service as he had a few scattered white hairs but he remembers he was brawny and unafraid. Isaac was too young but the other two uncles were accepted. One never returned because he was killed in battle but one fought throughout the war and was never wounded. He remembers how the white men were indignant because the negroes were allowed to enlist and how Mars Stanton Buckner was forced to hide out in the woods for many months because he had met slave Frank Buckner and hae tried to kill him. Frank returned to Greensburg, forgave his master and procurred a paper stating that he was at fault, afteh which Stanton returned to active service. "Yes, the road has been long. Memory brings back those days and the love of my mother is still real to me, God bless her!"

Relating to the value of an education Dr. Buckner hopes every Caucassian and Afro-American youth and maiden will strive to attain great heights. His first efforts to procure knowledge consisted of reciting A.B.S.s from the McGuffy's Blue backed speller with his unlettered sister for a teacher. In later years he attended a school conducted by the

Ex-Slave Stories
District #5
Vanderburgh County
Lauana Creel   A Slave, Ambassador and City Doctor.

P5. 31

Freemen's Association. He ✗ bought a grammar from a white school boy
and studied it at home. When sixteen years of age he was employed
to teach negro children and grieves to recall how limited his ability
was bound to have been. "When a father considers sending his son or
daughter to school, today, he orders catalogues, consults his friends
and considers the location and surroundings and the advice of those
who have patronized the different schools. He finally decides upon
the school that promises the boy or girl the most attractive and comfortable surroundings. When I taught the African children I boarded
with an old man whose cabin was filled with his own family. I climbed
a ladder leading from the cabin into a dark uncomfortable loft where
a comfort and a straw bed were my only conveniences."

Leaving Greensburg the young mulatto made his way to Indianapolis
where he became acquainted with the first educated negro he had ever
met. The negro was Robert Bruce Bagby, then principal of the only
school for negroes in Indianapolis. "The same old building is standing there today that housed Bagby's institution then," he declares.

Dr. Buckner recalls that when he left Bagby's school he was so
low financially he had to procure a position in a private residence as
house boy. This position was followed by many jobs of serving tables
at hotels and eating houses, of any and all kinds. While engaged in
that work he met Colonel Albert Johnson and his lovely wife, both natives of Arkansas and he remembers their congratulations when they learned that he was striving for an education. They advised his entering
an educational institution at Terre Haute. His desire had been to
enter that institution of Normal Training but felt doubtful of succeed-
ing in the advanced courses taught because his advantages had been so
limited, but Mrs. Johnson told him that "God gives his talents to the

A Slave, Ambassador and City Doctor.

different species and kix he would love and protect the negro boy."

After studying several years at the Terre Haute State Normal
George W. Buckner felt assured that he was reasonably prepared to
teach the negro youths and accepted the professorship of £ schools
at Vincennes, Washington and other Indiana Villages. "I was interested
nu in the young people and anxious for their advancement but the suffering endured by my invalid mother, Who had passed into the great beyond, and the memory of little Master Dickie's lingering illness and
untimely death would not desert my consciousness. I determined to take
up the study of medical practice and surgery which I did."

Dr. Buckner graduated from the Indiana Electic Medical College in
1890. His services were needed at Indianapolis so he practiced medicine
in that city for a year, then located at Evansville where he has enjoyed an ever increasing popularity on account of his sympathetic attitude
among his people.

"When I came to Evansville," says Dr. Buckner, "there were seventy white physicians practicing in the area, they are now among the de-
parted. Their task was streneous, roads were almost impossible to
travel and those brave men soon sacrificed their lives for the good of
suffering humanity."   Dr. Buckner described several of the old doc-
tors as "Striding a horse and setting out through all kinds of weather."

Dr. Buckner is a veritable encyclopedia of negro lore. He stops
at many points during an interview to relate stories he has gleaned
here and there. He has forgotten where he first heard this one or
that one but it helps to illustrate a point. One he heard near the
end of the war follows, and although it has recently been retold it X
holds the interest of the listener. "Andrew Jackson owned an old negro
slave, who stayed on at the old home when his beloved master went into

politics, became an American soldier and statesman and finally the 7th president of the United States.   The good slave still remained through the several years of the quiet uneventful last years of his master and witnessed his death, which occurred at his home near Nashville, Tennessee. After the master had been placed under the sod, Uncle Sammy was seen each eay visiting Jackson's grave.

"Do you think President Jackson is in heaven?" an ay acquaintance asked Uncle Sammy.

"If-n he wanted to go dar, he dar now," said the old man. "If-n Mars Andy wanted to do any thing all Hell couldn't keep him from doin' it."

Dr. Buckner believes each negro is confident that he will take himself with all his peculiarities to the land of promise. Each physical feature and habitual idiosyncrasy will abide in his redeemed personality. Old Joe will be there in person with the wrinkle crossing the bridge of his nose and little stephen will wear his wool pulled back from his eyes and each will recognize his fellow man. "What fools we all are." declared Dr. Buckner.

Asked his views concerning the different books embraced in the Holy Bible, Dr. Buckner, who is a student of the Bible said, "I believe almost every story in the Bible is an allegory, composed to illustrate some fundemental truth that could otherwise never have been clearly presented only through the medium of an allegory."

"The most treacherous impulse of the human nature and the one to be most dreaded is jealousy." With these words the aged Negro Doctor launched into the expression of his political views. "I'm a Democrat." He then explained how he voted for the man but had confidence that his chosen party possesses ability in choosing proper candidates. He is an ardent follower of Franklin D. Roosevelt and speaks of Woodrow Wilson with bated breath.

Through the influence of John W. Boehne, Sr., and the friendly
advice of other influential citizens of Evansville Dr. Buckner was ap-
pointed minister to Liberia, on Woodrow Wilson's cabinet, in the year
1913. Dr. Buckner appreciated the confidence of his friends in appoint-
ing him and cherishes the experineces gained while abroad. He noted
the expressions of gratitude toward cabinet members by the citizens of
that African coast. One Albino youth brought an offering of luscious
mangoes and desired to see the minister from the United States of America.
Some natives presented palm oils. "The natives have been made to understand that the United States has given aid to Liberia in a financial way
and the customs - service of the republic is temporarily administered
headed by an American." "A thoroughly civilized negro state does not
exist in Liberia nor do I believe in any part of West Africa. Superstit--
tion is the interpretation of their religion, their poritical views are
a hodgepodge of unconnected ideas. Strangth over rules knowledge and
jealousy crowds out almost all hope of sympathetic achievement and ad-
justment." Dr. Buckner recounted incidents where jealousy was apparant
in the behavior of men and women of higher civilizations than the African natives.   While voyaging to Spain on board a Spanish vessel, he
witnessed a very refined,polite Jewish woman being reduced to tears by
the taunts of a Spanish officer, on account of her nationality. "Jealousy," he said, "protrudes itself into politics, religion and prevents
educational achievement. "

"During a political campaign I was compelled to pay a robust negro man to follow me about my professional visits and my social evenings
with my friends and family, to prevent meeting physical violence to
myself or family when political factions were virtually at war within
the area of Evansville. The influence of political captains had brought
about the dreadful condition and ignorant negroes responded to their

A Slave, Ambassador and City Doctor.

political graft, without realizing who had befriended them in need."

"The negro youths are especially subject to propoganda of the four-flusher for their home influence is, to say the least, negative. Their opportunities limited, their education neglected and they are easily aroused by the meddling influence of the vote-getter and the traitor. I would to God that their eyes might be opened to the light."

Dr. Buckner's influence is mostly exhibited in the sick room, where his presence is introduced in the effort to relieve pain.

The gradual rise from slavery to prominence, the many trials encountered along the road has ripened the always sympathetic nature of Dr. Buckner into a responsive suffer among a suffering people. He has hope that proper influences and sympathetic advice will mould the plastic character of the Afro-American youths of the United States into proper citizens and that their immortal souls inherit the promised reward of the redeeemed through grace.

"Receivers of emancipation from slavery and enjoyers of emancipation from sin through the sacrifice of Abraham Lincoln and Jesus Christ; Why should not the negroes be exalted and happy?" are the words of Dr. Buckner.

Note: G. W. Buckner was born December 1st, 1852. The negroes in Kentucky expressed it , "In fox huntin' time" One brother was born in "Simmon time", one in "Sweet tater time," and another in "Plantin' time."

-----Negro lore .

Ex-Slave Stories
District #5
Vanderburgh County
Lauana Creel

1300321

The Life Story of George Taylor Burns.

(Personal Interview)

Ox-carts and flat boats, and pioneer surroundings; crowds of men and women crowding to the rails of river steamboats; gay ladies in holiday attire and gentleman in tall hats, low cut vests and silk mufflers; for the excursion boats carried the gentry of every area.

A little negro boy clung to the ragged skirts of a slave mother, both were engrossed in watching the great wheels that ploughed the Mississippi river into foaming billows. Many boats stopped at Gregery's Landing, Missouri to stow away wood, for many engines were fired with wood in the early days.

The Burns brothers operated a wood yard at the Landing and the work of cutting, hewing and piling wood for the commerce was performed by slaves of the Burns plantation.

George Taylor Burns was five years of age and helped his mother all day as she toiled in the wood yards. "The colder the weather, the more hard work we had to do." declares Uncle George.

George Taylor Burns, the child of Missouri slave parents, recalls the scenes enacted at the Burns' wood yards so long ago. He is a resident of Evansville, Indiana and his snow white hair and beard bears testimony that his days have been already long upon the earth.

Uncle George remembers the time when his infant hands reached in vain for his mother, the kind and gentle Lucy Burns: Remembers a long cold winter of snow and ice when boats were tied up to their moorings. Old master died that winter and many slaves were sold by the heirs, among them was Lucy Burns. Little George clung to his mother but strong hands tore away his clasp. Then he watched her cross a distant hill, chained to a long line of departing slaves. George never saw his parents again and although the memory of his mother is vivid he scarcely remembers his father's face. He said, "Father was black but my mother was a bright mulatto."

Ex-Slave Stories
District #5
Vanderburgh County   The Life Story of George Taylor Burns.
Lauana Creel.

2.
37

Nothing impressed the little boy with such unforgettable imagery as the cold which descended upon Greogery's Landing one winter.   Motherless, hungry, desolate and unloved, he often cried himself to sleep at night while each day he was compelled to carry wood.   One morning he failed to come when the horn was sounded to call the slaves to breakfast.   "Old Missus went to the negro quarters to see what was wrong." and "She was horrified when she found I was frozen to the bed."

She carried the small bundle of suffering humanity to the kitchen of her home and placed him near the big oven.   When the warmth thawed the frozen child the toes fell from his feet.   "Old Missus told me I would never be strong enough to do hard work, and she had the neighborhood shoemaker fashion shoes too short for any body's feet but mine." said Uncle George.

Uncle George doesn't remember why he left Missouri but the sister of Greene Taylor brought him to Troy, Indiana.   Here she learned that she could not own a slave within the State of Indiana so she indentured the child to a flat boat captain to wash dishes and wait on the crew of workers.

George was so small of stature that the captain had a low table and stool made that he might work in comfort.   George's mistress received $15.00 per month for the service of the boy for several years.

From working on the flat boats George became accustomed to the river and soon received employment as a cabin boy on a steam boat and from that time through out the most active days of his life George Taylor Burns was a steam-boat man. In fact he declares, "I know steamboats from wood box to stern wheel."

"The life of a riverman is a good life and interesting things happen on the river." says Uncle George.

Uncle George has been imprisoned in the big jail at New Orleans. He has seen his fellow slaves beaten into insensibility while chained to the whipping post in Congo Square at New Orleans.

He was badly treated while a slave but he has witnessed even more cruel treatment administered to his fellow slaves.

Among other exciting occurrences remembered by the old negro man when he recalls early river adventures is one in which a flat boad sunk near New Orleans. After clinging for many hours to the drifting wreckage he was rescued, half dead from exhaustion.

In memory, George Taylor Burns stands in the slave mart at New Orleans and hears the Auctioneers' hammer, for he was sold like a beast of burden by Greene Taylor, brother of his mistress. Greene Taylor, however, had to refund the money and return the slave to his mistress when his crippled feet were discovered.

"Greene Taylor was like many other people I have known. He was always ready to make life unhappy for a negro."

Uncle George, although possessing an unusual amount of intelligence and ability to learn, has a very limited education. "The negroes were not allowed an education," he relates. "It was dangerous for any person to be caught teaching a negro and several negroes were put to death because they could read."

Uncle George recalls a few superstitions entertained by the rivermen. "It was bad luck for a white cat to come aboard the boat." "Horse shoes were carried for good luck." "If rats left the boat the crew was uneasy, for fear of a wreck." Uncle George has very little faith in any superstition but remembers some of the crews had.

Among other boats on which this old river man was employed are "The Atlantic" on which he was cabin boy. The "Big Gray Eagle" on which he assisted in many ways. He worked where boats were being constructed while he lived at New Albany.

Many soldiers were returned to their homes by means of flat boats and steam boats when the Civil War had ended and many recruits were sent by water during the war. Just after peace was declared George met Elizabeth Slye, a young slave girl who had just been set free. "Liza would come to see her mother who was

District #5
Vanderburgh County
Lauana Creel   The Life Story of George Taylor Burns.

page 4.
39

working on a boat." "People used to come down to the landings to see boats come in,"said Uncle George.   George and Liza were free, they married and made New Albany their home, until 1881 when they came to Evansville.

Uncle George said the Eclipse was a beautiful boat, he remembers the lettering in gold and the bright lights and polished rails of the longest steam boat ever built in the west. Measuring 365 feet in length and Uncle George declares, "For speed she just up and hustled."

"Louisville was one of the busiest towns in the Ohio Valley." says Uncle George, but he remembers New Orleans as the market place where almost all the surpleus products were marketed.

Uncle George has many friends along the water-front towns.   He admires the Felker family of Tell City, Indiana. He is proud of his own race and rejoices in their opportunities, He remembers his fear of the Ku Kluxs, his horror of the patrol and other clans united to make life dangerous for newly emancipated negroes

George Taylor Burns draws no old age pension. He owns a building located at Canal and Evans Streets that xx houses a number of negro families. He is glad to say his credit is good in every market in the city.   Although lamed by rhumatic pains and hobbling on feet toeless from his young childhood he has led a useful life. "Don't forget I knew Pilot Tom Ballard, and Aaron Ballard on the Big Eagle in 1858," warns Uncle George. "We Negroes carried passes so we could save our skins if we were caught off the boats but we had plenty of good food on the boats."

Uncle George said the roust-abouts sang gay songs while loading boats with heavy freight and provisions but on account of his crippled feet he could not be a roust-about.

Federal Writers' Project   Page #1
    of the W. P. A.   Topic #240
    District #6   Anna Pritchett
Marion County
File #60-A

Folklore

References

    (A) Mrs. Belle Butler -daughter-

                829 North Capitol avenue.

    (B) Anna Pritchett -Federal Writer-

                1200 Kentucky Avenue.

        Belle Butler, the daughter of Chaney Mayer, tells of the hardships her mother endured during her days of slavery. (B)

        Chaney was owned by Jesse Coffer, "a mean old devil." He would whip his slaves for the slightest misdemeanor, and many times for nothing at all -just enjoyed seeing them suffer. Many a time Jesse would whip a slave, throw him down, and gouge his eyes out. Such a cruel act! (A)

        Chaney's sister was also a slave on the Coffer plantation. One day their master decided to whip them both. After whipping them very hard, he started to throw them down, to go after their eyes. Chaney grabbed one of his hands, her sister grabbed his other hand, each girl bit a finger entirely off of each hand of their master.

This, of course, hurt him so very bad he had to stop their punishment and never attempted to whip them again. He told them he would surely put them in his pocket (sell them) if they ever dared to try anthing like that again in life. (A)

Not so long after their fight, Chaney was given to a daughter of their master, and her sister was given to another daughter and taken to Passaic County, N.C. (A)

On the next farm to the Coffer farm, the overseers would tie the slaves to the joists by their thumbs, whip them unmercifully, then salt their backs to make them very sore. (A)

When a slave slowed down on his corn hoeing, no matter if he were sick, or just very tired, he would got many lashes and a salted back. (A)

One woman left the plantation without a pass. The overseer caught her and whipped her to death. (A)

No slave was ever allowed to look at a book, for fear he might learn to read. One day the old mistress caught a slave boy with a book, she cursed him and asked him what he meant, and what he thought he could do with a book. She said he looked like a black dog with a breast pin on, and forbade him to ever look into a book again. (A)

All slaves on the Coffer plantation were treated in a most inhuman manner, scarcely having enough to eat, unless they would steal it, running the risk of being caught and receiving a severe beating for the theft. (A)

Mrs. Butler lives with her daughters, has worked very hard in "her days." (B)

She has had to give up almost everything in the last few years, because her eyesight has failed. However, she is very cheerful and enjoys telling the "tales" her mother would tell her. (B)

Submitted December 28, 1937
Indianapolis, Indiana

By: ANNA PRITCHETT
         Field Writer

Joseph William Carter.

This information was gained through an interview with Joseph William Carter and several of his daughters. The data was cheerfully given to the writer. Joseph William Carter has lived a long and, he declares, a happy life, although he was born and reared in bondage, and his pleasing personality has always made his lot an easy one and his yoke seemed easy to wear.

Joseph William Carter was born prior to the year 1836. His mother, Malvina Gardner was a slave in the home of Mr. Gardner until a man named D. B. Smith saw her and noticing the physical perfection of the child at once purchased her from her master.

Malvina was agrieved.at being compelled to leave her old home, and her love-ly young mistress, Puss Gardner was fond of the little mullato girl and had taught her to be a useful member of the Gardner family; however, she was sold to Mr. Smith and was compelled to accompany him to his home.

Both the Gardner and Smith families lived near Gallatin, Tennessee, in Sumner County. The Smith plantation was situated on the Cumberland River and commanded a beautiful view of river and valley acres but Malvina was very unhappy. She did not enjoy the Smith family and longed for her old friends back in the Gardner home.

One night the little girl gathered together her few personal belongings and started back to her old home.

Afraid to travel the highway the child followed a path she knew through the forest; but alas, she found the way long and beset with perils. A number of uncivil Indians were encamped on the side of the Cumberland moun-tains and a number of the young braves were out hunting that night. Their stealthy approach was heard by the little fugitive girl but too late for her to make an escape. An Indian called "Buck" captured her and by all the laws of the tribe she was his own property. She lived for almost a year in the

Joseph William Carter.

teepe with Buck and during that time learned much about Indian habits.

When Malvina was missed from her new home, Mr. Smith went to the Gardner plantation to report his loss, not finding her there a wide search was made for her but the Indians kept her thoroughly concealed.   Miss Puss, however, kept up the search. She knew the Indians were encamped on the mountain and believed she would find the girl with them.   The Indians finally broke camp and the members of the Gardner home watched them start on their journey and Miss Puss soon discovered Malvina among the other maidens in the procession.

The men of the Gardner plantation ,white and black, overtook the Indians and demanded the girl be given up to them.   The Indians reluctantly gave her to them. Miss Puss Gardner took her back and Mr. Gardner paid Mr. Smith the original purchase price and Malvina was once more installed in her old home.

Malvina Gardner was not yet twelve years of age when she was captured by the Indians and was scarcely thirteen years of age when she became the mother of Joseph William, son of the uncivil Indian, "Buck".   The child was born in the Gardner home and mother and child remained there.   The mother was a good slave and loved the members of the Gardner family and her son and she were loved by them in return.

Puss Gardner married a Mr. Mooney and Mr. Gardner allowed her to take Joseph William to her home.   The Mooney estate was situated up on the Carth- ridge road and some of Joseph William's most vivid memories of slavery and the curse of bondage embrace his life's span with the Mooneys.

One story that the aged man relates is of an encounter with an eagle and follows: "George Irish, a white boy near my own age, was the son of the miller. His father operated a sawmill on Bledsoe Creek near where it empties into the Coumberland river. George and I often went fishing together and

x-Slave Stories
th District
Vanderburgh County
Lauana Creel.

Joseph William Carter.

page 3. 45

had a good dog called Hector. Hector was as good a coon dog as there
was to be found in that part of the country. That day we boys climbed up
on the mill shed to watch the swans in Bledsoe Creek and we soon noticed a
great big fish hawk catching the goslings. It made us mad and we decided
to kill the hawk. I went back to the house and got an old flint lock rifle
Marse Mooney had let me carry when we went hunting. When I got back where
George was, the big bird was still busy catching goslings. The first shot
I fired broke its wing and I decided I would catch it and take it home with
me. The bird put up a terrible fight, cutting me with its bill and talons.
Hector came running and tried to help me but the bird cut him until his
howls brought help from the field. Mr. Jacob Greene was passing along and
came to us. He tore me away from the bird but I could not walk and the blood
was running from my body in dozens of places. Poor old Hector, was crippled
and bleeding for the bird was a big eagle and would have killed both of us
if help had not come!' The old negro man still shows signs of his encounter
with the eagle. He said it was captured and lived about four months in cap-
tivity but its wing never healed. The body of the eagle was stuffed with
wheat bran, by Greene Harris, and placed in the court yard in Sumner County.
The Civil War changed things at the Mooney plantation," said the old man.
"Before the War Mr. Mooney never had been cruel to me. I was Mistress Puss's
property and she would never have allowed me to be abused, but some of the
other slaves endured the most cruel treatment and were worked nearly to death
        Uncle Joe's memory of slavery embraces the whole story of bondage and
the helpless position held by strong bodied men and women of a hardy race,
overpowered by the narrow ideals of slave owners and cruel overseerers.
"When I was a little bitsy child and still lived with Mr. Gardner," said
the old man, "I saw many of the slaves beaten to death. Master Gardner
didn't do any of the whippin' but every few months he sent to Mississippi

Ex-slave Stories
5th District
Vanderburgh County
Indiana
Lauana Creel.

Joseph William Carter.

page 4.

46

for negro rulers to come to the plantation and whip all the negroes that had not obeyed the overseers.   A big barrel lay near the barn and that was always the whippin place." Uncle Joe remembers two or three profession-al slave whippers and recalls the death of two of the Mississippi whippers. He relates the story as follows: "Mars Gardner had one of the finest black smiths that I ever saw. His arms were strong, his muscles stood out on his breast and shoulders and his legs were never tired. He stood there and shoed horses and repaired tools day after day and there was no work ever made him tired."

The old negro man so vividly described the noble blacksmith that he almost appeared in person, as the story advanced.   "I don't know what he had done to rile up Mars Gardner, but all of us knew that the Blacksmith was going to be flogged.   When the whippers from Mississippi got to the plantation. The blacksmith worked on day and night. all day he was shoein horses and ll the spare time he had he was makin a knife.   When the whippers got there ll of us were brought out to watch the whippin but the blacksmith, Jim ardner did not wait to feel the lash, he jumped right into the bunch of overseers and negro whippers and knifed two whippers and one overseer to eath; then stuck the sharp knife into his arm and bled to death."

Suicide seemed the only hope for this man of strength. He could not humble imself to the brutal ordeal of being beaten by the slave whippers.

When the war started, we kept hearing about the soldiers and finally they et up their camp in the forest near us. The corn was ready to bring into e barn and the soldiers told Mr. Mooney to let the slaves gather it and t it into the barns. Some of the soldiers helped gather and crib the orn. I wanted to help but Miss Pyss was afraid they would press me into ervice and made me hide in the cellar. There was a big keg of apple cider

in the cellar and every day Miss Puss handed down a big plate of fresh
ginger snaps right out of the oven, so I was well fixed."   The old man
remembers that after the corn was in the crib the soldiers turned in their
horses to eat what had fallen to the ground.

Before the soldiers became encamped at the Mooney plantation they had camp--
ed upon a hill and some skirmishing had occurred.   Uncle Joe remembers the
skirmish and seeing cannon balls come over the fields.   The cannon balls
were chained together and the slave children would run after the missils.
Sometimes the chains would cut down trees as the balls rolled through the
forest.

"Do you believe in witchcraft?" was asked while interviewing the aged negro.
"No was the answer.   "I had a cousin that was a full blooded Indian and a
Voo doo doctor.   He got me to help him with his Voo doo work.   A lot of
people both white and black sent for the Indian when they were sick.   I told
him I would do the best I could, if it would help sick people to get well.
A woman was sick with rhumatism and he was going to see her.   He sent me into the woods to dig up poke roots to boil.   He then took the brew to the
house where the sick woman lived.   Had her to put both feet in a tub filled
with warm water , into which he had placed the poke root brew.   He told
the woman she had lizards in her body and he was going to bring them out of
her.   He covered the woman with a heavy blanket and made her sit for a ling
time, possibly an hour, with her feet in the tub of poke root brew and water.
He had me slip a good many lizards into the tub and when the woman removed
her feet, there were the lizards.   She was soon well and believed the lizards had come out of her legs.   I was disgusted and would not practice with
my cousin again."

"So you didn't fight in the Civil War." was asked Uncle Joe.
Of course I did, when I got old enough I entered the service and barbacued

meat until the war closed." Barbacueing had been Uncle Joe's specialty
during slavery days and he followed the same profession during his service
with the federal army. He was freed by the emancuapation proclamation, and
soon met and married Sadie Scott, former Slave of Mr. Scott, a Tennessee
planter. Sadie only lived a short time after her marriage,. He later
married Amy Doolins. Her father was named Carmuel. He was a blacksmith
and after he was free, the countrymen were after him to take his life. He
was shot nine times and finally killed himself to prevent meeting death at
the hands of the clansmen.

Joseph William Carter is a cripple. In 1933 he fell and broke his right
thigh-bone and since that time he has walked with a crutch. He stays up
quite a lot and is always glad to welcome visitors. He possesses a noble
character and is admired by his friends and heighbors. Tall, straight,
lean of body, his nose is aquiline; these physical characteristics he in-
herited from his Indian ancesters. His gentle nature, wit, and good humor
are characteristics handed to him by his mother and fostered by the gentle
rearing of his southern mistress.

When Uncle Joe Carter celebrated the 100th aniversary of his birth a large
cake was presented to him. decorated with 100 candles. The party was attended by children and grandchildren, friends and neighbors. "What is your
political viewpoint?" was asked the old man.

"My politics is my love for my country". "I vote for the man, not the
party."

Uncle Joe's religion is the religion of decency and virtue. "I don't want to
be hard in my judgement,"said he,"But I wish the whole world would be decent.
When I was young man, women wore more clothes in bed than they now wear on
the street."

"Papa has always been a lover of horses but he does not care for Automobiles
nor aeroplanes." said a daughter of Uncle Joe. Uncle Joe has seven daugh-

x-Slaves Stories
5th District
anderburgh County
quana Creel

Joseph William Carter

Page 7.   49

rs, he says they have always been obedient and attentive to their parents.

heir mother passed away seven years ago. The sons and daughters of Uncle

e remember their grand-mother and recall stories recounted by her of her

ptivity among the Indians.

"Papa had no gray hairs until after mama died. His hair turned gray from

ief at her loss." said "rs. Della Smith, one of his daughters. Uncle Joe's

mile reveals a set of unusually sound teeth from which only one tooth is

issing.

ke all fathers and grandfathers, Uncle Joe recounts the cute deeds and fun-

sayings of the little children he has been associated with: how his own

ildren with feather bedecked crowns enacted the capture of their grandmother

nd often played "Voo-Doo Doctor." ··

ncle Joe stresses the value of work, not the enforced labor of the slave but

e cheerful toil of free people. He is glad that his sons and daughters

e industrious citizens and is proud they maintain clean homes for their fam-

lies. xHisxdaughtersxare He is happy because his children have never

nown bondage, and he respects the laws of his country and appreciates the

terest that the citizens of Evansville have always showed in the negro race.

    After Uncle Joe became a young man he met many indians from the tribe

at had held his mother captive. Through them he learned much about his

ther which his mother had never told him.

    Though he was a gardner slave and would have been Joseph Gardner, he took
                              is
e name of Carter from a step father and was known as Joseph Carter.

OHIO COUNTY EX-SLAVE, MRS. ELLEN CAVE, RELATES HER EXPERIENCES

Ref. (A) Assistant editor of "The Rising Sun Recorder" furnished the following story which had appeared in the paper, March 19, 1937.

Mrs. Cave was in slavery for twelve years before she was freed by the Emancipation Proclamation. When she gave her story to Aubrey Robinson she was living in a temporary garage home back of the Rising Sun courthouse having lost everything in the 1937 flood.

Mrs. Cave was born on a plantation in Taylor County Kentucky. She was the property of a man who did not live up to the popular idea of a Southern gentleman, whose slaves refused to leave them, even after their freedom was declared.

When she was a year old her mother was sold to someone in Louisana and she did not see her again until 1867, when they were re-united in Carrolton, Kentucky. Her father died when she was a baby.

Mrs. Cave told of seeing wagon loads of slaves sold down the river. She, herself was put on the block several times but never actually sold, although she would have preferred being sold rather than the continuation of the ordeal of the block.

Her master was a "mean man" who drank heavily, he had twenty slaves that he fed now and then, and gave her her freedom after the war only when she would remain silent about it no longer. He was a Southern sympathiser but joined the Union army where he became a captain and was in charge of a Union commissary. Finally he was suspected and charged with mustering supplies to the rebels. He was imprisoned for some time, then courtmartialed and sentenced to die. He escaped by bribing his negro guard.

Mrs. Cave said that her master's father had many young women slaves and sold his own half-breed children down the river to Louisiana plantations where the work was so severe that the slaves soon died.

While in slavery, Mrs. Cave worked as a maid in the house until she grew older when she was forced to do all kinds of outdoor labor. She remembered sawing logs in the snow all day. In the summer she pitched hay or any other man's work in the field. She was trained to carry three buckets of water at the same time, two in her ahands and one on her head and said she could still do it.

On this plantation the chief article of food for the slaves was bran-bread, although the master's children were kind and often slipped them out meat or other food.

Mrs. Cave remembered seeing General Woolford and General Morgan of the Southern forces when they made friendly visits to the plantation. She saw General Grant twice during the war. She saw soldiers drilling near the plantation. Later she was caught and whipped by night riders, or "pat-a-rollers", as she tried to slip out to negro religious meetings.

Mrs. Cave was driven from her plantation two years after the war and came to Carrollton Kentucky, where she found her mother and soon married James Cave, a former slave on a plantation near hers in Taylor county. Mrs. Cave had thirteen children.

For many years Mrs. Cave has lived on a farm about two and one half mi. south of Rising Sun. Everything she had was washed away in the flood and she lived in the court house garage until her home could be rebuilt. (A)

Federal Writers' Project   Page #1
 of the W. P. A.   Topic #240
 District #6   Anna Pritchett
Marion County
File #41-A

Folklore

References

   (A) Mrs. Harriet Cheatam -Ex-Slave, 816 Darnell street.

   (B) Anna Pritchett, Federal Writer, 1200 Kentucky Avenue.

   Incidents in the life of Mrs. Cheatam as she told them to me. (B)

   "I was born, in 1843, in Gallatin, Tennessee, 94 years ago this coming (1937) Christmas day." (A)

   "Our master, Martin Henley, a farmer, was hard on us slaves, but we were happy in spite of our lack." (A)

   "When I was a child, I didn't have it as hard as some of the children in the quarters, I always stayed in the "big house," slept on the floor, right near the fireplace, with one quilt for my bed and one quilt to cover me. Then when I growed up, I was in the quarters." (A)

   "After the Civil war, I went to Ohio to cook for General Payne. We had a nice life in the general's house." (A)

   "I remember one night, way back before the Civil war,

we wanted a goose. I went out to steal one as that was the only
way we slaves would have one. I crept very quiet-like, put my
hand in where they was and grabbed, and what do you suppose I had?
A great big pole cat. Well, I dropped him quick, went back, took off
all my clothes, dug a hole, and buried them. The next night I
went to the right place, grabbed me a nice big goose, held his neck
and feet so he couldn't holler, put him under my arm, and ran with him,
and did we eat?" (A)

"We often had prayer meeting out in the quarters, and to
keep the folks in the "big house" from hearing us, we would take
pots, turn them down, put something under them, that let the
sound go in the pots, put them in a row by the door, then our
voices would not go out, and we could sing and pray to our heart's
content." (A)

"At Thanksgiving time we would have pound cake. That
was fine. We would take our hands and beat and beat our cake
dough, put the dough in a skillet, cover it with the lid and put it
in the fireplace. (The covered skillet would act our ovens of
today." It would take all day to bake, but it sure would be good;
not like the cakes you have today." (A)

"When we cooked our regular meals, we would put our
food in pots, slide them on an iron rod that hooked into the fireplace. (They were called pot hooks.) The pots hung right over
the open fire and would boil until the food was done." (A)

"We often made ash cake. (That is made of biscuit dough.) When the dough was ready, we swept a clean place on the floor of the fireplace, smoothed the dough out with our hands, took some ashes, put them on top of the dough, then put some hot coals on top of the ashes, and just left it. When it was done, we brushed off the coals, took out the bread, brushed off the ashes, child, that was bread." (A)

"When we roasted a chicken, we got it all nice and clean, stuffed him with dressing, greased him all over good, put a cabbage leaf on the floor of the fireplace, put the chicken on the cabbage leaf, then covered him good with another cabbage leaf, and put hot coals all over and around him, and left him to roast. That is the best way to cook chicken." (A)

Mrs. Cheatam lives with a daughter, Mrs. Jones. She is a very small old lady, pleasant to talk with, has a very happy disposition. Her eyes, as she said, "have gotten very dim," and she can't piece her quilts anymore. That was the way she spent her spare time.

She has beautiful white hair and is very proud of it. (B)

Submitted December 1, 1937
Indianapolis, Indiana

By: ANNA PRITCHETT
Field Writer

Ex-Slave Tales
District #5
Vanderburgh County
Lauana Creel

130012

James Childress' Story.

55

From an interview with James Childress and from John Bell both living at 312 S. E. Fifth Street, Evansville, Indiana.

Known as Uncle Jimmy by the many children that cluster about the aged man never tiring of his stories of "When I was a chile."

"When I was a chile my daddy and mamma was slaves and I was a slave," so begins many recounted tales of the long ago.

Born at Nashville, Tennessee in the year 1860, Uncle Jimmie remembers the Civil War days with the exciting events as related to his own family and the family of James Childress, his master. He remembers sorrow expressed in parting tears when "Uncle Johnie and Uncle Bob started to war. He recalls happy days when the beautiful valley of the Cumberland was abloom with wild flowers and fertile acres were carpeted with blue grass.

"A beautiful view could always be enjoyed from the hillsides and there were many pretty homes belonging to the rich citizens, Slaves kept the lawns smooth and tended the flowers for miles around Nashville, when I was a child." said Uncle Jimmie.

Uncle Jimmie Childress has no knowledge of his master's having practiced cruelty towards any slave. "We was all well fed, well clothed and lived in good cabins. I never got a cross word from Mars John in my life," he declared. "When the slaves got their freedom they rejoiced staying up many nights to sing, dance and enjoy themselves, although they still depended on old Mars John for food and bed, they felt too excited to work in the fields or care for the stock. They hated to leave their homes but Mr. Childress told them to go out and make homes for themselves."

"Mother got work as a housekeeper and kept us all together. Uncle Bob got home from the War and we lived well enough. I have lived at

James Childress' Story.   a. 56

Evansville since 1881, have worked for a good many men and John Bell
will tell you I have had only friends in the city of Evansville."

Uncle Jimmie recalls how the slaves always prayed to God for
freedom and the negro preachers always preached about the day when the
slaves would be no longer slaves but free and happy.

"My people loved God, they sang sacred songs, 'Swing Low Sweet
Charriot' was one of the best songs they knew". Here uncle Jimmie
sang a stanza of the song and said it related to God's setting the
negroes free.

"The negroes at Mr. Childress' place were allowed to learn as
much as they could.   Several of the young men could read and write.
"Our master was a good man and did no harm to anybody."

James Childress is a black man, small of stature, with crisp
wooly dark hair. He is glad he is not a mulatto but a thorough
blooded negro.

Federal Writers' Project   Page #1
   of the W. P. A.   Topic #840
   District #6   Anna Pritchett
   Marion County
   <u>File #44-A</u>

Folklore

<u>References</u>

     (A) Mrs. Sarah Colbert -Ex-Slave- 1505 North Capitol

           avenue, Indianapolis, Indiana.

     (B) Anna Pritchett -Federal Writer- 1200 Kentucky Avenue.

        Mrs. Sarah Carpenter Colbert was born in Allen County,
Kentucky in 1855. She was owned by Leige Carpenter, a farmer. (A)

        Her father, Isaac Carpenter was the grandson of his
master, Leige Carpenter, who was very kind to him. Isaac worked
on the farm until the old master's death. He was then sold to Jim
McFarland in Frankfort Kentucky. Jim's wife was very mean to the
slaves, whipped them regularly every morning to start the day right.
(A)

        One morning after a severe beating, Isaac met an old slave,
who asked him why he let his mistress beat him so much. Isaac
laughed and asked him what he could do about it. The old man told
him if he would bite her foot, the next time she knocked him down,
she would stop beating him and perhaps sell him. (A)

        The next morning he was getting his regular beating, he
willingly fell to the floor, grabbed his mistress' foot, bit her

very hard. She tried very hard to pull away from him, he held on
still biting, she ran around in the room, Isaac still holding on.
Finally, she stopped beating him and never attempted to strike
him again. (A)

The next week he was put on the block, being a very good
worker and a very strong man, the bids were high. (A)

His young master, Leige Jr., outbid everyone and
bought him for $1200.00.

His young mistress was very mean to him. He went again to
his old friend for advice. This time he told him to get some
yellow dust, sprinkle it around in his mistress' room and if
possible, get some in her shoes. This he did and in a short time
he was sold again to Johnson Carpenter in the same county. He was
not really treated any better there. By this time he was very
tired of being mistreated. He remembered his old master telling
him to never let anyone be mean to him. He ran away to his old
mistress, told her of his many hardships, and told her what the
old master had told him, so she sent him back. At the next sale
she bought him, and he lived there until slavery was abolished. (A)

Her grandfather, Bat Carpenter, was an ambitious slave;
he dug ore and bought his freedom, then bought his wife by paying
$50.00 a year to her master for her. She continued to work on the
farm of her own master for a very small wage. (A)

Bat's wife, Matilda, lived on the farm not far from
him, he was allowed to visit her every Sunday. One Sunday,

it looked like rain, his master told him to gather in the oats,
he refused to do this and was beaten with a raw hide. He was so
angry, he went to one of the witch -crafters for a charm so he
could fix his old master. (A)

The witch doctor told him to get five new nails, as there
were five members in his master's family, walk to the barn, then
walk backwards a few steps, pound one nail in the ground, giving
each nail the name of each member of the family, starting with the
master, then the mistress, and so on through the family. Each
time one nail was pounded down in the ground, walk backwards and nail
the next one in until all were pounded deep in the ground. He
did as instructed and was never beaten again. (A)

Jane Garmen was the village witch. She disturbed the
slaves with her cat. Always at milking time the cat would appear,
and at night would go from one cabin to another, putting out the
grease lamps with his paw. No matter how they tried to kill
the cat, it just could not be done.

An old witch doctor told them to melt a dime, form a
bullet with the silver, and shoot the cat. He said a lead bullet
would never kill a bewitched animal. The silver bullet fixed the
cat. (A)

Jane also bewitched the chickens. They were dying so
fast anything they did seemed useless. Finally a big fire was
built and the dead chickens thrown into the fire, that burned the

charm, and no more chickens died. (A)

Mrs. Colbert lives with her daugher in a very
comfortable home. She seems very happy and was glad to talk of
her early days. How she would laugh when telling of the experiences of her family.

She has reared a large family of her own, and feels very
proud of them. (B)

Submitted December 1, 1937
Indianapolis, Indiana

By: ANNA PRITCHETT
            Field Writer

D183.. 4
Johnson County, Ind.
Wm. R. Mays
July 29, 1937
SLAVERY
753 words   61

SLAVERY DAYS OF MANDY COOPER OF
LINCOLN COUNTY, KENTUCKY

Ref: Frank Cooper, 715 Ott St., Franklin, Ind.

Frank Cooper, an aged colored man of Franklin, relates some very interesting conditions that existed in slavery days as handed down to him by his mother.

Mandy Cooper, the mother of Frank Cooper, was 115 years old when she died; she was owned by three different families: the Good's, the Burton's, and the Cooper's, all of Lincoln Co. Kentucky.

"Well, Ah reckon Ah am one of the oldest colored men hereabouts," confessed aged Frank Cooper. "What did you all want to see me about?" My mission being stated, he related one of the strangest categeries alluding to his mother's slave life that I have ever heard.

"One day while mah mammy was washing her back my sistah noticed ugly disfiguring scars on it. Inquiring about them, we found much to our amazement, that they were mammy's relics of the now gone, if not forgotten, slave days.

"This was her first reference to her "misery days" that she had evah made in my presence. Of course we all thought she was tellin' us a big story and we made fun of her. With eyes flashin', she stopped bathing, dried her back and reached for the smelly ole black whip that hung behind the kitchen door. Biddin' us to strip down to our waists, my little mammy with the boney bent-ovah back, struck each of us as hard as evah she could with that black-snake whip, each stroke of the whip drew blood from our backs. "Now", she said to us, "you have a taste of slavery days." With three of her children now having tasted of some of her "misery days" she was in the mood to tell us more of her sufferings; still indelibly impressed in my mind.

'My ole back is bent ovah from the quick-tempered blows feld by the red-headed Miss Burton.

'At dinner time one day when the churnin' wasn't finished for the noonday meal', she said with an angry look that must have been reborn in mah mammy's eyes -- eyes that were dimmed by years and hard livin', 'three white women beat me from anguh because they had no butter for their biscuits and cornbread. Miss Burton used a heavy board while the missus used a whip. While I was on my knees beggin' them to quit, Miss Burton hit the small of mah back with the heavy board. Ah knew no more until kind Mr. Hamilton, who was staying with the white folks, brought me inxide the cabin and brought me around with the camphor bottle. Ah'll always thank him - God bless him - he picked me up where they had left me like a dog to die in the blazin' noonday sun.

'After mah back was broken it was doubted whether ah would evah be able to work again or not. Ah was placed on the auction block to be bidded for so mah owner could see if ah was worth anything or not. One man bid $1700. after puttin' two dirty fingahs in my mouth to see my teeth. Ah bit him and his face showed angah. He then wanted to own me so he could punish me.

'Thinkin' his bid of $1700 was official he unstrapped his buggy whip to beat me, but my mastah saved me. My master declared the bid unofficial.

'At this auction my sister was sold for $1900 and was never seen by us again.'

"My mother related some experiences she had with the Paddy-Rollers, later called the "Kuklux", these Paddy-Rollers were a constant dread to the Negroes. They would whip the poor darkeys unmercifully without any cause. One night while the Negroes were gathering for a big party and dance they got wind of the approaching Paddy-Rollers in large numbers on horseback. The Negro men did not know what to do for protection, they became desperate and decided to gather a quantity of grapevines and tied them fast at a dark place in the road. When the Paddy-Rollers came thundering down the road bent on deviltry and unaware of the trap set for them, plunged head-on into these strong grapevines and three of their number were killed and a score was badly injured. Several horses had to be shot following injuries.

"When the news of this happening spread it was many months before the Paddy-Rollers were again heard of."

130170

Albert Strope, Field Worker   64
Federal Writers' Project
St. Joseph County — District #1
Mishawaka, Indiana

EX -SLAVES

REFERENCE

A - Rev. H. H. Edmunds,
     403 West Hickory Street
          Elkhart, Indiana

EX-SLAVE

REV. H. H. EDMUNDS

Rev. H. H. Edmunds has resided at 403 West Hickory Street
in Elkhart for the past ten years. Born in Lynchburg, Virginia,
in 1859, he lived there for several years. Later he was taken to
Mississippi by his master, and finally to Nashville, Tennessee,
where he lived until his removal to Elkhart.

Mr. Edmunds is very religious, and for many years has served his people as a minister of the Gospel. He feels deeply that
the religion of today has greatly changed from the "old time religion." In slavery days, the colored people were so subjugated
and uneducated that he claims they were especially susceptible
to religion, and poured out their religious feelings in the so-
called negro spirituals. Mr. Edmunds is convinced that the
superstitions of the colored people and their belief in ghosts
and gobblins is due to the fact that their emotions were worked
upon by slave drivers to keep them in subjugation. Oftentimes
white people dressed as ghosts, frightened the colored people
into doing many things under protest. The "ghosts" were feared
far more than the slave-drivers.

The War of the Rebellion is not remembered by Mr. Edmunds, but
he clearly remembers the period following the war known as the
Reconstruction Period. The negroes were very happy when they
learned they were free as a result of the war. A few took advantage of their freedom immediately, but many, not knowing
what else to do, remained with their former masters. Some remained on the plantations five years after they were free.

Gradually they learned to care for themselves, often through instructions received from their former masters, and then they were glad to start out in the world for themselves. Of course, there were exceptions, for the slaves who had been abused by cruel masters were only too glad to leave their former homes.

The following reminiscence is told by Mr. Edmunds:

"As a boy, I worked in Virginia for my master, a Mr. Farmer. He had two sons who served as bosses on the farm. An elder sister was the head boss. After the war was over, the sister called the colored people together and told them that they were no longer slaves, that they might leave if they wished.

"The slaves had been watering cucumbers which had been planted around barrels filled with soil. Holes had been bored in the barrels, and when water was poured in the barrels, it gradually seeped out through the holes thus watering the cucumbers.

"After the speech, one son told the slaves to resume their work. Since I was free, I refused to do so, and as a result, I received a terrible kicking. I mentally resolved to get even some day. Years afterward, I went to the home of this man for the express purpose of seeking revenge. However, I was received so kindly, and treated so well, that all thoughts of vengeance vanished. For years after, my former boss and I visited each other in our own homes."

Mr. Edmunds states that the negro people prefer to be referred to as colored people, and deeply resent the name "nigger."

Archie Koritz, Field Worker
Federal Writers' Project
Lake County - District #1
Gary, Indiana

67

EX-SLAVES

JOHN EUBANKS & FAMILY

REFERENCE

A - John Eubanks and family
Gary, Indiana

EX-SLAVES

John Eubanks & Family

Gary's only surviving Civil War veteran was born a slave in Barren County, Kentucky, June 6, 1836. His father was a mulatto and a free negro. His mother was a slave on the Everrett plantation and his grandparents were full-blooded African negroes. As a child he began work as soon as possible and was put to work hoeing and picking cotton and any other odd jobs that would keep him busy. He was one of a family of several children, and is the sole survivor, a brother living in Indianapolis, having died there in 1935.

Following the custom of the south, when the children of the Everrett family grew up, they married and slaves were given them for wedding presents. John was given to a daughter who married a man of the name of Eubanks, hence his name, John Eubanks. John was one of the more fortunate slaves in that his mistress and master were kind and they were in a state divided on the question of slavery. They favored the north. The rest of the children were given to other members of the Everrett family upon their marriage or sold down the river and never saw one another until after the close of the Civil War.

Shortly after the beginning of the Civil War, when the north seemed to be losing, someone conceived the idea of forming negro regiments and as an inducement to the slaves, they offered them freedom if they would join the Union forces. John's mistress and master told him that if he wished to join the Union forces, he had their consent and would not have to run away like other slaves were doing. At the beginning of the war, John was twenty-one years of age. When Lincoln freed the slaves by his Emancipation Proclamation, John was promptly given his freedom by his master and mistress.

John decided to join the northern army which was located at Bowling Green, Kentucky , a distance of thirty-five miles from Glasgow where John was living. He had to walk the entire thirty-five miles. Although he fails to remember all the units that he was attached to, he does remember that it was part of General Sherman's army. His regiment started with Sherman on his famous march through Georgia, but for some reason unknown to John, shortly after the campaign was on its way, his regiment was recalled and sent elsewhere.

His regiment was near Vicksburg, Mississippi, at the time Lee surrendered. Since Lee was a proud southerner and did not want the negroes present when he surrendered, Grant probably for this reason as much as any other refused to accept Lee's sword. When Lee surrendered there was much shouting among the troops and John was one of many put to work loading cannons on boats to be shipped up the river. His company returned on the steamboat "Indiana." Upon his return to Glasgow, Ky. he saw for the first time in six years, his mother and other members of his family who had returned free.

Shortly after he returned to Glasgow at the close of the Civil War, he saw several colored people walking down the highway and was attracted to a young colored girl in the group who was wearing a yellow dress. Immediately he said to himself, "If she ain't married there goes my wife." Sometime later they met and were married Christmas day in 1866. To this union twelve children were born four of whom are living today, two in Gary and the others in the south.

After his marriage he lived on a farm near Glasgow for several years, later moving to Louisville, where he worked in a lumber yeard.   He came to Gary in 1924, two years after the death of his wife.

President Grant was the first president for whom he cast his vote and he continued to vote until old age prevented him from walking to the polls.

Although Lincoln is one of his favorite heroes, Teddy Roosevelt tops his list of great men and he never failed to vote for him.

In 1926, he was the only one of three surviving memebers of the Grand Army of the Republic in Gary and mighty proud of the fact that he was the only one in the parade.   In 1937 he is the sole survivor.

He served in the army as a member of Company K of the 108th, Kentucky Infantry (Negro Volunteers).

When General Morgan, the famous southern raider, crossed the Ohio on his raid across southern Indiana, John was one of the negro fighters who after heavy fighting, forced Morgan to recross the river and retreat back to the south.   He also participated in several skirmishes with the cavalry troops commanded by the famous Nathan Bedfored Forrest, and was a member of the negro garrison at Fort Pillow, on the Mississippi which was assaulted and captured.   This resulted in a massacre of the negro soldiers.   John was in several other fights, but as he says, "never onct got a skinhurt."

At the present time, Mr. Eubanks is residing with his daughter, Mrs. Bertha Sloss and several grandchildren, in Gary, Indiana.   He is badly crippled with rheumatism, has poor eyesight and his memory is failing.   Otherwise his health is good.   Most of his teeth are good and they are a source of wonder to his dentist.   He is ninety-

eight years of age and his wish in life now, is to live to be a
hundred.   Since his brother and mother both died at ninety-eight
and his paternal grandfather at one hundred-ten years of age, he
has a good chance to realize this ambition.

Because of his condition most of this interview was had from
his grandchildren, who have taken notes in recent years of any
incidents that he relates. He is proud that most of his fifty
grandchildren are high school graduates and that two are attending
the University of Chicago.

In 1935, he enjoyed a motor trip, when his family took him
back to Glasgow for a visit.   He suffered no ill effects from the
trip.

AD: DB
10-5-37

EX-SLAVES

INTERVIEW WITH JOHN EUBANKS, EX-SLAVE

A - Archie Koritz, Field Worker
816 Mound Street
Valparaiso, Indiana

John Eubanks, Gary's only negro Civil War survivor has lived
to see the ninety-eighth anniversary of his birth and despite his
advanced age, recalls with surprising clarity many interesting and
sad events of his boyhood days when a slave on the Everett plantation.

He was born in Glasgow, Barron County, Kentucky, June 6, 1839,
one of seven children of a chattel of the Everett family.

The old man retains most of his faculties, but bears the mark
of his extreme age in an obvious feebleness and failing sight and
memory.   He is physically large, says he once was a husky, weighing
over two hundred pounds, bears no scars or deformities and despite
the hardships and deprivations of his youth, presents a kindly and
tolerant attitude.

"I remembah well, us young uns on the Everett plantation,"
he relates, "I worked since I can remembah, hoein', pickin' cotton
and othah chohs 'round the fahm.   We didden have much clothes,
nevah no undahweah, no shoes, old ovahalls and a tattahed shirt,
wintah and summah.   Come de wintah, it be so cold mah feet weah
plumb numb mos' o' de time and manya time - when we git a chanct-
we druve the hogs from outin the bogs an' put ouah feet in the
wahmed wet mud.   They was cracked and the skin on the bottoms and
in de toes weah cracked and bleedin' mos' o' time, wit bloody scabs
but de summah healed them agin."

"Does yohall remembah, Granpap," his daughter prompted, "
Yoh mahstah - did he treat you mean?"

"No," his tolerant acceptance apparent in his answer,
"it weah done thataway. Slaves weah whipt and punished and the
younguns belonged to the mahstah to work foah him oh to sell. When

I weah 'bout six yeahs old, Mahstah Everett give me to Tony
Eubanks as a weddin' present when he married mahstah's daughtah
Becky.   Becky would'n let Tony whip her slaves who came from
her fathah's plantation.   'They ah my prophty,' she say, 'an'
you caint whip dem.'   Tony whipt his othah slaves but not Becky's."

      "I remembah" he continued, "how they tied de slave 'round a
post, wit hands tied togedder 'round the post, then a husky lash
his back wid a snakeskin lash 'til hisn back were cut and bloodened,
the blood spattered" gesticulating with his unusually large hands,
"an' hisn back all cut up.   Den they'd pouh salt watah on hem.   Dat
dry and hahden and stick to hem.   He nevah take it off 'till it
heal.   Sometimes I see marhstah Everett hang a slave tip-toe.   He
tie him up so he stan' tip-toe an' leave him thataway.

      "I be twenty-one wehn wah broke out.   Mahstah Eubanks say to
me, 'Yohall don' need to run 'way ifn yohall want to jine up wid de
ahmy.'   He say, 'Deh would be a fine effin slaves run off.   Yohall
don' haf to run off, go right on and I do not pay dat fine.'   He
say, ''nlist in de ahmy but don' run off.'   Now I walk thirty-five
mile from Glasgow to Bowling Green to dis place - to de 'nlistin'
place - from home fouh mile - to Glasgow - to Bowling Green, thirty-
five mile.   On de road I meet up with two boys, so we go on.   Dey
run 'way from Kentucky, and we go together.   Then some Bushwackers come
down de road.   We's scared and run to the woods and hid.   As we run
tru de woods, pretty soon we heerd chickens crowing.   We fill ouah
pockets wit stones.   We goin' to kill chickens to eat.   Pretty soon
we heerd a man holler, 'You come 'round outta der'- and I see a white
man and come out.   He say, 'What yoh all doin' heah?'   I turn 'round
and say, 'Well boys, come on boys.'   an' the boys come out.   The man

say, 'I'm Union Soldier. What yoh all doin' heah?' I say, 'We goin'
to 'nlist in de ahmy.' He say, 'Dat's fine' and he say, 'come 'long'
He say, 'git right on white man's side'- we go to station. Den he
say, 'You go right down to de station and give yoh inforhmation. We
keep on walkin'. Den we come to a white house wit stone steps in front
so we go in. An' we got to 'nlistin' place and jine up wit de ahmy.

"Den we go trainin' in d' camp and we move on. Come to a little
town ..... a little town. We come to Bolling Green.. den to Louisville.
We come to a rivah ..... a rivah (painfully recalling) d' Mississippi.

"We weah 'nfantry and petty soon we gits in plenty fights, but
not a scratch hit me. We chase dem cavalry. We run dem all night
and next mohnin' d' Captain he say, 'Dey done broke down.' When we
rest, he say 'See dey don' trick you.' I say, 'We got all d' ahmy
men togedder. We hold dem back 'til help come.'

"We don' have no tents. Sleep on naked groun' in wet and cold
and rain. Mos' d' time we's hungry but we win d' war and Mahstah
Eubanks tell us we no moah hisn property, we's free now.'

The old man can talk only in short sentences and his voice dies
to a whisper and soon the strain became evident. He was tired. What
he does remember is with surprising clearness especially small details,
but with a helpless gesture, he dismisses names and locations. He
remembers the exact date of his discharge, March 20, 1866, which his
daughter verified by producing his discharge papers. He remembers
the place, Vicksburg, the Company - K, and the Regiment, 180th.
Dropping back once more to his childhood he spoke of an incident which
his daughter says makes them all cry when he relates it, although they
have heard it many times.

"Mahstah Everett whipt me onct and mothah she cried. Then
Mahstah Everett say, 'Why yoh all cry? - Yoh cry I whip anothah of
these young uns. She try to stop. He whipt 'nother. He say, 'Ifn
yoh all don' stop, yoh be whipt too! ' and mothah she trien to stop
but teahs roll out, so Mahstah Everett whp her too.

"I wanted to visit mothah when I belong to Mahst' Eubanks, but
Becky say, 'Yoh all best not see youh mothah, or yoh wan ' to go
all de time' then explaining, 'she wan' me to fohgit mothah, but I
nevah could.   When I cm back from d' ahmy, I go home to mothah
and say 'don' y' know me?' She say, 'No, I don' know you.' I say,
'Yoh don' know me?' She say, 'No, ah don' know yoh.'   I say, I'se
John.' Den she cry and say how ahd growd and she thought I'se daid
dis long time.   I done 'splain how the many fights I'se in wit no
scratch and she bein' happy."

Speaking of Abraham Lincoln's death, he remarked, "Sho now, ah
remembah dat well. We all feelin' sad and all d' soldiers had wreaths
on der guns."

Upon his return from the army he married a young negress he had
seen some time previous at which time he had vowed some day to make her
his wife. He was married Christmas day, 1866.   For a number of years
he lived on a farm of his own near Glasgow. Later he moved with his
family to Louisville where he worked in a lumber yard.   In 1923, two
years after the death of his wife, he came to Gary, when he retired.
He is now living with his daughter, Mrs. Sloss, 2713 Harrison Boulevard,
Gary.

Interview with Mr. John W. Fields, Ex-Slave
of Civil War period. September 17, 1937

John W. Fields, 2120 North Twentieth Street, Lafayette, Indiana,
now employed as a domestic by Judge Burnett is a typical example of
a fine colored gentlemen, who, despite his lowly birth and adverse
circumstances, has labored and economezed until he has acquired a
respected place in his home community. He is the owner of three
properties, un-mortgaged, and is a member of the colored Baptist Church of
Lafayette. As will later be seen his life has been one of constant
effort to better himself spiritually and physically. He is a fine
example of a man who has lived a morally and physically clean life.
But, as for his life, I will let Mr. Fields speak for himself:

"My name is John W. Fields and and I'm eighty-nine(89) years old. I
was born March 27, 1848 in Owensburg, Ky, thats 115 miles below
Louisville, Ky. There was 11 other children besides myself in my family.
When I was six years ofd, all of us children were taken from my
parents, because my master died and his estate had to be settled.
We slaves were divided by this method. Three disinterested persons were
chosen to come to the plantation and together they wrote the names
of the different heirs on a few slips of paper. These slips were put in
a hat and passed among us slaves. Each one took a slip and the name
on the slip was the new owner. I happened to draw the name of a
relative of my master who was a widow. I can't describe the heart-
break and horror of that separation. I was only six years ofd and it
was the last time I ever saw my mother for longer than one night. Twelve

children taken from my mother in one day. Five sisters and two brothers
went to Charleston, Virginia, one brother and one sister went to Lexington,
Ky., one sister went to Hartford, Ky., and one brother and myself
stayed in Owensburg, Ly. My mother was later allowed to visit amoung
us children for one week of each year, so she could only remain a short
time at each place.

"My life prior to that time was filled with heart-aches and des-
pair. We arose from four to five O'clock in the morning and parents
and children were given hard work, lasting until nightfall gaves us
our respite. After a meager supper, we generally talked until we
grew sleepy, we had to go to bed. Some of us would read, if we were
lucky enough to know how.

"In most of us colored folks was the great desire to able to read
and write. We took advantage of every opportunity to educate ourselves.
The greater part of the plantation owners were very harsh if we were
caught trying to learn or write. It was the law that if a white man
was caught try to educate a negro slave, he was liable to prosecution
entailing a fine of fifty dollars and a jail sentence. We were never allowed
to go to town and it was not until after I ran away that I knew that they
sold anything but slaves, tobacco and wiskey. Our ignorance was the
greatest hold the South had on us. We knew we could run away, but what
then? An offender guilty of this crime was subjected to very harsh
punishment.

"When my masters estate had been settled, I was to go with the widowed
relative to her place, she swung me up on her horse behind her and promised me all manner of sweet things if I would come peacefully. I didn't
fully realize what was happening, and before I knew it , I was on my
way to my new home. Upon arrival her manner changed very much, and she took
me down to where there was a bunch of men burning brush. She said: "see these

men?" I said; yes. Well, so help them, she replied. So at the age of six
I started my life as an independent slave. From then on my life as a slave
was a repetition of hard work, poor quarters and board. We had no beds
at that time, we just "bunked" on the floor. I had one blanket and manys the
night I sat by the fireplace during the long cold nights in the winter.

My Mistress had separated me from all my family but one brother
with sweet words, but that pose was dropped after she reached her place.
Shortly after I had been there, she married a northern man by the name of
David Hill. At first he was very nice to us, but he gradually acquired
a mean and overbearing manner toward us. I remember one incident that
I don't like to remember. One of the women slaves had been very sick and
she was unable to work just as fast as he thought she ought to. He had driven
her all day with no results. That night after completeing our work he
called us all together. He made me hold a light, while he whipped her
and then made one of the slaves pour salt water on her bleeding back. My
innerds turn yet at that sight.

At the beginning of the Civil War I was still at this place
as a slave. It looked at the first of the war as if the south would
win, as most of the big battles were won by the South. This was because
we slaves stayed at home and tended the farms and kept their families.

To eliminate this solid support of the South, the Emancipation
Act was passed, freeing all slaves. Most of the slaves were so ignorant
they did not realize they were free. The planters knew this and as
Kentucky never seceeded from the Union, they would send slaves into
Kentucky from other states in the south and hire them out to plantations.
For these reasons I did not realize that I was free untill 1864. I immediately
resolved to run away and join the Union Army and so my brother and I went to

Owensburg, Ky. and tried to join. My brother was taken, but I was refused as being too young. I reide at Evansville, Terre Haute and Indianapolis
but was unable to get in. I then tried to find work and was finally
hired by a man at $7.00 a month. That was my first independent job.
From then on I went from one job to another working as general laborer.

I married at 24 years of age and had four children. My wife has
been dead for 12 years and 8 months. Mr. Miller, always remembere that:
                "The brightest man, the prettiest flower
                May be out down, and withered in an hour."

Today, I am the only surviving member who helped organize the second
Baptist Church here in Lafayette, 64 years ago. I've tried to live according to the way the Lord would wish, God Bless you.

                "The clock of Life is wound but once.
                Today is yours, tonorrow is not,
                No one knows when the hands will stop."

NEGRO FOLKLORE

MR. JOHN FIELDS, EX-SLAVE, 2120

N. 20th. ST. LAFAYETTE, INDIANA.

Mr. Fields says that all negro slaves were ardent believers in ghosts, supernatual powers,, tokens and "signs." The following story illustrates the point.

"A turkey gobbler had mysteriously disappeared from one of the neighboring plantations and the local slaves were accused of commeting the fowl to a boiling pot. A slave convicted of theft was punished severly. As all of the slaves denied any knowledge of the turkey's whereabouts, they were instructed to make a search of the entire plantation."

"On one part of the place there was a large peach orchard. At the time the trees were full of the green fruit. Under one of the trees was a large cabinet or "safe" as they were called. One of the slaves accidently opened the safe and, Behold, there was Mr. Gobbler peacefully seated on a number of green peaches.

"The negro immediately ran back and notified his master of the discovery. The master returned to the orchard with the slave to find that the negro's wild tale was true. A turkey gobbler sitting on a nest of green peaches A bad omen.

"The master had a son who had been seriously injured some time before by a runaway team, and a few days after this unusual occurence with the turkey, the son died. After his death, the word of the turkey's nesting venture and the deate of the master's son spread to the four winds, and for some time after this story was related wherever there was a public gathering with the white people or the slave population."

All through the south a horseshoe was considered an omen of good luck. Rare indeed was the southern home that did not have one nailed over the door. This insured the household and all who entered of plesant prospects while within the home. If while in the home you should perhaps get into a violent argument, never hit the other party with a broom as it was a sure indication of bad luck. If Grandad had the rheumatics, he would be sure of relief if he carried a buckeye in his pocket.

Of all the Ten Commandments, the one broken most by the negro was: Thou Shalt Not Steal This was due mostly to the insufficient food the slaves obtained. Most of the planters expected a chicken to suddenly get heavenly aspirations once in a while, but as Mr. Fields says, "When a beautiful 250 pound hog suddenly tries to kidnap himself, the planter decided to investigate." It occured like this:

"A 250 pound hog had been fruitless. The planter was certain that the culprit was among his group of slaves, so he decided to personally conduct a quiet investigation.

One night shortly after the moon had risen in the sky, two of the negroes were seated at a table in one of the cabins talking of the experiences of the day. A knock sounded on the door. Both slaves jumped up and cautiously peeked out of the window. Lo! there was the master patiently waiting for an answer. The visiting negro decided that the master must not see both of them and he asked the other to conceal him while the master was there. The other slave told him to climb into the attic and be perfectly quiet. When this was done, the tenant of the cabin answered the door.

The master strode in and gazed about the cabin. He then

turned abruptly to the slave and growled, 'Alright, where is that
hog you stoled? 'Massa, replied the negro, 'I know nothing about no
hog. The master was certain that the slave was lying and told him so
in no uncertain terms. The terrified slave said, 'Massa, I know nothing
of any hog. I never seed him. The Good Man up above knows I never
seed him. HE knows every thing and HE knows I didn't steal him!
The man in the attic by this time was aroused at the misunderstood
conversation taking place below him. Disregarding all, he raised his
voice and yelled, 'He's a liar, Massa, he knows just as much about it
as I do!

Most of the strictly negro folklore has faded into the past.
The younger negro generations who have been reared and educated in the
north have lost this bearing and assumed the lore of the local white
population through their daily contact with the whites. The older
negro natives of this section are for the most part employed as
domestics and through this channel rapidly assimilated the employers
viewpoint in most of his beliefs and conversations.

INDIANS MADE SLAVES AMONG THE NEGROES

Interviews with George Fortman. Cor. Bellemeade Ave. and Garvin St.,
Evansville, Indiana, and other interested citizens.

"The story of my life, I will tell to you with sincerest respect to
all and love to many, although reviewing the dark trail of my childhood and
early youth causes me great pain." So spoke George Fortman, an aged man and
former slave, although the history of his life reveals that no Negro blood
runs through his veins.

"My story necessarily begins by relating events which occurred in
1838, when hundreds of Indians were rounded up like cattle and driven away
from the valley of the Wabash. It is a well known fact recorded in the histories of Indiana that the long journey from the beautiful Wabash Valley was
a horrible experience for the fleeing Indians, but I have the tradition as
relating to my own family, and from this enforced flight ensued the tragedy
of my birth."

The aged ex-slave reviews tradition. "My two ancestors, John Hawk,
a Blackhawk Indian brave, and Racheal, a Chackatau maiden had made themselves
a home such as only Indians know, understand and enjoy. He was a hunter and
a fighter but had professed faith in Christ through the influence of the
missionaries. My greatgrandmother passed the facts on to her children and
they have been handed down for four generations. I, in turn, have given the
traditions to my children and grandchildren.

"No more peaceful home had ever offered itself to the red man than the
beautiful valley of the Wabash river. Giant elms, sycamores and maple trees
bordered the stream while the fertile valley was traversed with creeks and
rills, furnishing water in abundance for use of the Indian campers.

"The Indians and the white settlers in the valley transacted business
with each other and were friendly towards each other, as I have been told by
my mother, Eliza, and my grandmother, Courtney Hawk.

"The missionaries often called the Indian families together for the
purpose of teaching them and the Indians had been invited, prior to being
driven from the valley, to a sort of festival in the woods. They had prepared
much food for the occasion. The braves had gone on a long hunt to provide
meat and the squaws had prepared much corn and other grain to be used at the
feast. All the tribes had been invited to a council and the poor people
were happy, not knowing they were being deceived.

"The decoy worked, for while the Indians were worshiping God the meeting was rudely interrupted by orders of the Governor of the State. The Governor, whose duty it was to give protection to the poor souls, caused them to
be taken captives and driven away at the point of swords and guns.

"In vain, my grandmother said, the Indians prayed to be let return to
their homes. Instead of being given their liberty, some several hundred
horses and ponies were captured to be used in transporting the Indians away
from the valley. Many of the aged Indians and many innocent children died
on the long journey and traditional stories speak of that journey as the
'trail of death.' "

"After long weeks of flight, when the homes of the Indians had been
reduced to ashes, the long trail still carried them away from their beautiful
valley. My greatgrandfather and his squaw became acquainted with a party of
Indians that were going to the canebrakes of Alabama. The pilgrims were not
well fed or well clothed and they were glad to travel towards the south, believing the climate would be favorable to their health.

"After a long and dreary journey, the Indians reached Alabama. Rachael
had her youngest papoose strapped on to her back while John had cared for the

larger child, Lucy. Sometimes she had walked beside her father but often she had become weary or sleepy and he had carried her many miles of the journey, besides the weight of blankets and food. An older daughter, Courtney, also accompanied her parents.

"When they neared the cane lands they heard the songs of Negro slaves as they toiled in the cane. Soon they were in sight of the slave quarters of Patent George's plantation. The Negroes made the Indians welcome and the slave dealer allowed them to occupy the cane house; thus the Indians became slaves of Patent George.

"Worn out from his long journey John Hawk became too ill to work in the sugar cane. The kindly-disposed Negroes helped care for the sick man but he lived only a few months. Rachel and her two children remained on the plantation, working with the other slaves. She had nowhere to go. No home to call her own. She had automatically become a slave. Her children had become chattel.

"So passed a year away, then unhappiness came to the Indian mother, for her daughter, Courtney, became the mother of young Master Ford George's child. The parents called the little half-breed "Eliza" and were very fond of her. The widow of John Hawk became the mother of Patent George's son, Patent Junior.

"The tradition of the family states that in spite of these irregular occurrences the people at the George's southern plantation were prosperous, happy, and lived in peace each with the others. Patent George wearied of the Southern climate and brought his slaves into Kentucky where their ability and strength would amass a fortune for the master in the iron ore regions of Kentucky.

"With the wagon trains of Patent and Ford George came Rachel Hawk and her daughters, Courtney, Lucy and Rachel. Rachel died on the journey from Alabama but the remaining full blooded Indians entered Kentucky as slaves.

"The slave men soon became skilled workers in the Hillman Rolling
Mills. Mr. Trigg was owner of the vast iron works called the "Chimneys" in
the region, but listed as the Hillman, Dixon, Boyer, Kelley and Lyons Furnaces.
For more than a half century these chimneys smoked as the most valuable devel-
opment in the western area of Kentucky. Operated in 1810, these furnaces
had refined iron ore to supply the United States Navy with cannon balls and
grape shot, and the iron smelting industry continued until after the close of
the Civil War.

"No slaves were beaten at the George's plantation and old Mistress
Hester Lam allowed no slave to be sold. She was a devoted friend to all.

"As Eliza George, daughter of Ford George and Courtney Hawk, grew
into young womanhood the young master Ford George went oftener and oftener
to social functions. He was admired for his skill with firearms and for
his horsemanship. While Courtney and his child remained at the plantation
Ford enjoyed the companship of the beautiful women of the vicinity. At last
he brought home the beautiful Loraine, his young bride. Courtney was stoical
as only an Indian can be. She showed no hurt but helped Mistress Hester and
Mistress Loraine with the house work."

Here George Fortman paused to let his blinded eyes look back into the
long ago. Then he again continued with his story of the dark trail.

"Mistress Loraine became mother of two sons and a daughter and the
big white two-story house facing the Cumberland River at Smith Landing,
Kentucky, became a place of laughter and happy occasions, so my mother told
me many times.

"Suddenly sorrow settled down over the home and the laughter turned
into wailing, for Ford George's body was found pierced through the heart and
the half-breed, Eliza, was nowhere to be found.

"The young master's body lay in state many days. Friends and neighbors
came bringing flowers. His mother, bowed with grief, looked on the still face

of her son and understood -- understood why death had come and why Eliza
had gone away.

"The beautiful home on the Cumberland river with its more than 600
acres of productive land was put into the hands of an administrator of estates
to be readjusted in the interest of the George heirs. It was only then Mistress Hester went to Aunt Lucy and demanded of her to tell where Eliza could
be found.

'"She has gone to Alabama, Ole Mistus", said Aunt Lucy, 'Eliza was
scared to stay here.' A party of searchers were sent out to look for Eliza.
They found her secreted in a cane brake in the low lands of Alabama nursing
her baby boy at her breast. They took Eliza and the baby back to Kentucky.
I am that baby, that child of unsatisfactory birth."

The face of George Fortman registered sorrow and pain, it had been
hard for him to retell the story of the dark road to strange ears.

"My white uncles had told Mistress Hester that if Eliza brought me
back they were going to build a fire and put me in it, my birth was so unsatisfactory to all of them, but Mistress Hester always did what she believed
was right and I was brought up by my own mother.

"We lived in a cabin at the slave quarters and mother worked in the
broom cane. Mistress Hester named me Ford George, in derision, but remained
my friend. She was never angry with my mother. She knew a slave had to submit
to her master and besides Eliza did not know she was Master Ford George's
daughter."

The truth had been told at last. The master was both the father of
Eliza and the father of Eliza's son.

"Mistress Hester believed I would be feeble either in mind or body
because of my unsatisfactory birth, but I developed as other children did and
was well treated by Mistress Hester, Mistress Lorainne and her children.

"Master Patent George died and Mistress Hester married Mr. Lam,
while slaves kept working at the rolling mills and amassing greater wealth
for the George families.

"Five years before the outbreak of the Civil War Mistress Hester called
all the slaves together and gave us our freedom. Courtney, my grandmother,
kept house for Mistress Lorainne and wanted to stay on, so I too was kept at
the George home. There was a sincere friendship as great as the tie of blood
between the white family and the slaves. My mother married a negro ex-slave
of Ford George and bore children for him. Her health failed and when Mistress
Puss, the only daughter of Mistress Lorainne, learned she was ill she persuaded
the Negro man to sell his property and bring Eliza back to live with her."

"Why are you called George Fordman when your name is Ford George?"
was the question asked the old man.

"   "When the Freedsmen started teaching school in Kentucky the census
taker called to enlist me as a pupil. 'What do you call this child?' he asked
Mistress Lorainne. 'We call him the Little Captain because he carried himself
like a soldier,' said Mistress Lorainne. 'He is the son of my husband and a
slave woman but we are rearing him.' Mistress Lorainne told the stranger that
I had been named Ford George in derision and he suggested she list me in the
census as George Fordsman, which she did, but she never allowed me to attend
the Freedmen's School, desiring to keep me with her own children and let me be
taught at home. My mother's half brother, Patent George allowed his name to
be reversed to George Patent when he enlisted in the Union Service at the outbreak of the Civil War."

Some customs prevalent in the earlier days were described by George
Fordman. "It was customary to conduct a funeral differently than it is con-
ducted now," he said. "I remember I was only six years old when old Mistress
Hester Lam passed on to her eternal rest. She was kept out of her grave several

days in order to allow time for the relatives, friends and ex-slaves to be

notified of her death.

"The house and yard were full of grieving friends. Finally the lengthy
procession started to the graveyard. Within the George's parlors there had
been Bible passages read, prayers offered up and hymns sung, now the casket was
placed in a wagon drawn by two horses. The casket was covered with flowers
while the family and friends rode in ox carts, horse-drawn wagons, horseback,
and with still many on foot they made their way towards the river.

When we reached the river there were many canoes busy putting the
people across, besides the ferry boat was in use to ferry vehicles over the
stream. The ex-slaves were crying and praying and telling how good granny had
been to all of them and explaining how they knew she had gone straight to
Heaven, because she was so kind -- and a Christian. There were not nearly
enough boats to take the crowd across if they crossed back and forth all day,
so my mother, Eliza, improvised a boat or 'gunnel", as the craft was called,
by placing a wooden soap box on top of a long pole, then she pulled off her
shoes and, taking two of us small children in her arms, she paddled with her
feet and put us safely across the stream. We crossed directly above Iaka,
Livingston county, three miles below Grand River.

"At the burying ground a great crowd had assembled from the neighborhood across the river and there were more songs and prayers and much weeping.
The casket was let down into the grave without the lid being put on and everybody walked up and looked into the grave at the face of the dead woman. They
called it the 'last look' and everybody dropped flowers on Mistress Hester as
they passed by. A man then went down and nailed on the lid and the earth was
thrown in with shovels. The ex-slaves filled in the grave, taking turns with
the shovel. Some of the men had worked at the smelting furnaces so long that
their hands were twisted and hardened from contact with the heat. Their

shoulders were warped and their bodies twisted but they were strong as iron men from their years of toil. When the funeral was over mother put us across the river on the gunnel and we went home, all missing Mistress Hester.

"My cousin worked at Princeton, Kentucky, making shoes. He had never been notified that he was free by the kind emancipation Mrs. Hester had given to her slaves, and he came loaded with money to give to his white folks. Mistress Lorainne told him it was his own money to keep or to use, as he had been a free man several months.

"As our people, white and black and Indians, sat talking they related how they had been warned of approaching trouble. Jack said the dogs had been howling around the place for many nights and that always presaged a death in the family. Jack had been compelled to take off his shoes and turn them soles up near the hearth to prevent the howling of the dogs. Uncle Robert told how he believed some of Mistress Hester's enemies had planted a shrub near her door and planted it with a curse so that when the shrub bloomed the old woman passed away. Then another man told how a friend had been seen carrying a spade into his cousin's cabin and the cousin had said, 'Daniel, what foh you brung that weapon into by cabin? That very spade will dig my grave,' and sure enough the couxsin had died and the same spade had been used in digging his grave.

"How my childish nature quailed at hearing the superstitions discussed, I cannot explain. I have never believed in witbhcraft nor spells, but I remember my Indian grandmother predicted a long, cold winter when she noticed the pelts of the coons and other furred creatures were exceedingly heavy. When the breastbones of the fowls were strong and hard to sever with the knife it was a sign of a hard, cold and snowy winter. Another superstition was this: 'A green winter, a new graveyard - a white winter, a green graveyard.'

George Fortman relates how, when he accompanied two of his cousins into the lowlands ---there were very many Katy-dids in the trees --- their voices formed a nerve-racking orchestra and his cousin told him to tiptoe to the trees and touch each tree with the tips of his fingers. This he did, and for the rest of the day there was quiet in the forest.

"More than any other superstition entertained by the slave Negroes, the most harmful was the belief on conjurors. One old Negro woman boiled a bunch of leaves in an iron pot, boiled it with a curse and scattered the tea therein brewed, and firmly believed she was bringing destruction to her enemies. 'Wherever that tea is poured there will be toil and troubles,' said the old woman.

"The religion of many slaves was mostly superstition. They feared to break the Sabbath, feared to violate any of the Commandments, believing that the wrath of God would follow immediately, blasting their lives.

"Things changed at the George homestead as they change everywhere," said George Fortman. "When the Civil War broke out many slaves enlisted in hopes of receiving freedom. The George Negroes were already free but many thought it their duty to enlist and fight for the emancipation of their fellow slaves. My mother took her family and moved away from the plantation and worked in the broom cane. Soon she discovered she could not make enough to rear her children and we were turned over to the court to be bound out.

"I was bound out to David Varnell in Livingston County by order of Judge Busch and I stayed there until I was fifteen years of age. My sister learned that I was unhappy there and wanted to see my mother, so she influenced James Wilson to take me into his home. Soon goodhearted Jimmy Wilson took me to see Mother and I went often to see her."

Sometimes George would become stubborn and hard to control and then Mr. Wilson administered chastisement. His wife could not bear to have the boy punished. 'Don't hit him, Jimmie, don't kick him,' would say the good Scotch woman, who was childless. 'If he does not obey me I will whip him,' James

Wilson would answer. So the boy learned the lesson of obedience from the old couple and learned many lessons in thrift through their examples.

"In 1883 I left the Wilson home and began working and trying to save some money. River trade was prosperous and I became a 'Roustabout.' The life of the roustabout varied some with the habits of the roustabout and the disposition of the mate. We played cards, shot dice and talked to the girls who always met the boats. The 'Whistling Coon' was a popular song with the boatmen and one version of 'Dixie Land.' One song we often sang when nearing a port was worded 'Hear the trumpet Sound' --

> Hear the trumpet sound,
> Stand up and don't sit down,
> Keep steppin' 'round and 'round,
> Come jine this elegant band.
>
> If you don't step up and jine the bout,
> Old Massus sure will fine it out,
> She'll chop you in the head wid a golen ax,
>   You never will have to pay de tax,
>   Come jine the roust-a-bout band."

From roust-a-bout George became a cabin boy, cook, pilot, and held a number of positions on boats, plowing different streams. There was much wild game to be had and the hunting season was always open. He also remembers many wolves, wild turkeys, catamounts and deer in abundance near the Grand River. "Pet deer loafed around the milking pens and ate the feed from the mangers" said he.

George Fortman is a professor of faith in Christ. He was baptized in Concord Lake, seven miles from Clarksville, Tennessee, became a member of the Pleasant Greene Church at Callwell, Kentucky and later a member of the Liberty Baptist Church at Evansville.

"I have always kept in touch with my white folks, the George family," said the man, now feeble and blind. "Four years ago Mistress Puss died and I was sent for but was not well enough to make the trip home."

Too young to fight in the Civil War, George was among those who watched the work go on. 'I lived at Smiths Landing and remember the battle at Fort Donnelson. It was twelve miles away and a long cinder walk reached from the fort for nearly thirty miles. The cinders were brought from the iron ore mills and my mother and I have walked the length of it many times." Still reviewing the long, dark trail he continued. "Boatloads of soldiers passed Smith's Landing by day and night and the reports of cannon could be heard when battles were fought. We children collected Munnie balls near the fort for a long time after the war."

Although the George family never sold slaves or separated Negro families, George Fortman has seen many boats loaded with slaves on the way to slave marts. Some of the George Negroes were employed as pilots on the boats. He also remembers slave sales where Negroes were auctioned by auctioneers, the Negroes stripped of clothes to exhibit their physique.

"I have always been befriended by three races of people, the Caucassian, the African, and the Negro," declares George Fortman. "I have worked as a farmer, a river man, and been employed by the Illinois Central Railroad Company and in every position I have held I have made loyal friends of my fellow workmen." One friend, treasured in the memory of the aged ex-slave is Ollie James, who once defended George in court.

George Fortman has friends at Dauson Springs, Grayson Springs, and other Kentucky resorts. He has been a citizen of Evansville for thirty-five years and has had business connections here for sixty-two years. He janitored for eleven years for the Lockyear Business College, but his days of usefulness are over. He now occupies a room at Bellemeade Ave. and Garvin St. and his only exercise consists of a stroll over to the Lincoln High School. There he enjoys listening to the voices of the pupils as they play about the campus. "They are free", he rejoices. "They can build their own destinies, they did not arrive in this life by births of unsatisfactory circumstances. They have

the world before them and my grandsons and granddaughters are among them."

Federal Writers' Project
of the W. P. A.
District #6
Marion County
File #66-A

Page #1
Topic #240
Anna Pritchett

96

Folklore

References

(A) John Henry Gibson -Ex-slave- Colton Street.

(B) Anna Pritchett -Federal Writer- 1200 Kentucky Avenue.

John Henry Gibson was born a slave, many years ago, in Scott County, N.C. (A)

His old master, John Henry Bidding, was a wealthy farmer; he also owned the hotel, or rooming house. (A)

When court was in session, the "higher ups" would come to this house, and stay until the court affairs were settled. (A)

Mr. Bidding, who was very kind to his slaves, died when John Gibson was very young. All slaves and other property passed on to the son, Joseph Bidding, who in turn was as kind as his father had been. (A)

Gibson's father belonged to General Lee Gibson, who was a neighboring farmer. He saw and met Miss Elizabeth Bidding's maid; they liked each other so very much, Miss Elizabeth bought him from General Gibson, and let him have her maid as his wife. The wife lived only a short time, leaving a little boy. (A)

After the Civil war, a white man, by the name of Luster, was comming to Ohio, brought John Gibson with him. They came to Indianapolis, and Gibson liked it so well, he decided to remain; Mr. Luster told him if he ever became dissatisfied to come on to Ohio to him, but he remained in Indianapolis until 1872, then went back south, married, came back, and made Indianapolis his home. (A)

Mr. Gibson is very old, but does not know his exact age. He fought in the Civil war, and said he could not be very young to have done that. (B)

His sight is very nearly gone, can only distinguish light and dark. (B)

He is very proud of his name, having been named for his old master. (B)

Submitted January 24, 1938
Indianapolis, Indiana

By: ANNA PRITCHETT
          Field Writer

Submitted by:
William Webb Tuttle
District No. 2
Muncie, Indiana

NEGRO SLAVES IN DELAWARE COUNTY
MRS. BETTY GUWN

Reference: Mrs. Mattie Cash, daughter, resideing at 1101
East Second street, Muncie, Indiana.

Mrs. Betty Guwn was born March 25, 1832, as a slave on a tobacco
plantation, near Canton, Kentucky. It was a large plantation whose
second largest product was corn. She was married while quite young
by the slave method which was a form of union customary between the
white masters. If the contracting parties were of different plantations
the masters of the two estates bargained and the one sold his rights
to the one on whose plantation they would live. Her master bought
her husband, brought him and set them up a shack. Betty was the
personal attendant of the mistress. The home was a large Colonial
mansion and her duties were many and responsible. However, when
her house duties were caught up her mistress sent her immediately to
the fields. Discipline was quite stern there and she was "lined up"
with the others on several occasions.

Her cabin home began to fill up with children, fifteen in all.
The ventilation was ample and the husband would shoot a prowling dog
from any of the four sides of the room without opening the door. The
cracks between the logs would be used by cats who could step in any-
where. The slaves had "meetin'" some nights and her mistress would
call her and have her turn a tub against her mansion door to keep
out the sound.

Her master was very wealthy. He owned and managed a cotton farm
of two thousand acres down in Mississippi, not far from New Orleans.
Once a year he spent three months there gathering and marketing his

cotton. When he got ready to go there he would call all his slaves
about him and give them a chance to volunteer. They had heard awful
tales of the slave auction block at New Orleans, and the Master would
solemnly promise them that they should not be sold if they went down
of their own accord. "My Mistress called me to her and privately told
me that when I was asked that question I should say to him: "I will
go." The Master had to take much money with him and was afraid of
robbers. The day they were to start my Mistress took me into a private
room and had me remove most of my clothing; she then opened a strong
box and took out a great roll of money in bills; these she strapped
to me in tight bundles, arranging them around my waist in the circle
of my body. She put plenty of dresses over this belt and when she
was through I wore a bustle of money clear around my belt. I made
a funny "figger" but no one noticed my odd shape because I was a
slave and no one expected a slave to "know better". We always got
through safely and I went down with my Mistress every year. Of course
my husband stayed at home to see after the family, and took them to
the fields when too young to work under the task master, or over-seer.
Three months was a long time to be separated."

"When the Civil War came on there was great excitement among
we slaves. We were watched sharply, especially soldier timber for
either army. My husband ran away early and helped Grant to take
Fort Donaldson. He said he would free himself, which he did; but
when we were finally set free all our family prepared to leave. The
Master begged us to stay and offered us five pounds of meal and two
pounds of pork jowl each week if we would stay.and work. We all
went to Burgard, Kentucky, to live. At that time I was about 34
years old. My husband has been dead a long time and I live with my

children. If the "Good Lord" spares me until next March the 25th,

I will be 106 years old. I walk all about lively without crutches

and eye-glasses and I have never been sick until this year when a

tooth gave me trouble; but I had it pulled."

Arcmie Morris, Field Worker
Federal Writers' Project
Porter County - District #1   101
Valparaiso, Indiana

EX-SLAVES

REFERENCE

A - Mrs. Hockaday
       2581 Madison Street
              Gary, Indiana

EX-SLAVES

Mrs. Hockaday

Mrs. Hockaday is the daughter of an ex-slave and like so many others does not care to discuss the dark side of slavery and the cruel treatment that some of them received.

After the Civil War the slaves who for the most part were unskilled and ignorant, found it very difficult to adjust themselves to their new life as free persons. Formerly, they lived on the land of their masters and although compelled to work long hours, their food and lodging were provided for them. After their emancipation, this life was changed. They were free and had to think for themselves and make a living. Times for the negro then was much the same as during the depression. Several of the slaves started out to secure jobs, but all found it difficult to adjust themselves to the new life and difficult to secure employment. Many came back to their old owners and many were afraid to leave and continued on much as before.

The north set up stores or relief stations where the negro who was unable to secure employment could obtain food and shelter. Mrs. Hockaday says it was much the same as conditions have been the last few years.

About all the negro was skilled at was servant work and when they came north, they encountered the same difficulties as several of the colored folks who, driven by the terrible living conditions in the south four years ago, came to Gary. Arriving here they believed they were capable of servant work. However they were not accustomed to modern appliances and found it very difficult to adjust themselves. It was the same after the Emancipation.

Many owners were kind and religious and had schools for their slaves, where they could learn to read and write. Those slaves were more successful in securing employment.

Although the negro loved the Bible most of all books, and were mostly Methodists and Baptists, their different religious beliefs is caused by the slave owners having churches for the slaves. Whatever church the master belonged to, the slaves belonged to, and continued in the same church after the war.

Since slaves took the name of their owners, children in the same family would have different names. Mr. Hockaday's father and his brothers and sisters all had different names. On the plantation they were called "Jones' Jim," "Brown's Jones," etc. Many on being freed left their old homes and adopted any name that they took a fancy to. One slave that Mrs. Hockaday remembers took the name of Green Johnson and says he often remarked that he surely was green to adopt such a name. His grandson in Cary is an exact double for Clark Gable, except he is brown, and Gable is white.

Many slave owners gave their slaves small tracts of land which they could tend after working hours. Anything raised belonged to them and they could even sell the products and the money was theirs. Many slaves were able to save enough from these tracts to purchase their freedom long before the Emancipation.

Another condition that confronted the negro in the north was that they were not understood like they were by the southern people. In the south they were trusted and considered trustworthy by their owners. Even during the Civil War, they were trusted with the family jewels, silver, etc., when the northern army came marching

by, whereas in the north, even though they freed the slaves, they
would not trust them. For that reason many of the slaves did not
like the northern people and remained or returned to the southern
plantations.

The slave owners thought that slavery was right and nothing
was wrong about selling and buying human beings if they were
colored, much as a person would purchase a horse or automobile
today. The owners who whipped their slaves usually stripped
them to the waist and lashed them with a long leather whip,
commonly called a blacksnake.

Mrs. Hockaday is a large, pleasant, middle-aged woman and
does not like to discuss the cruel side of slavery and only recalls in a general way what she had heard old slaves discuss.

AD:DB
10-8-37

Federal Writers' Project
of the W. P. A.
District #6
Marion County
File #58-A

Page #1
Topic #240
Anna Pritchett

105

Folklore

Reference

(A) Robert Howard -Ex-slave, 1840 Boulevard Place.

(B) Anna Pritchett, Federal Writer, 1200 Kentucky Avenue.

Robert Howard, an ex-slave, was born in 1852, in Clara County, Kentucky. (A)

His master, Chelton Howard, was very kind to him. (A)

The mother, with her five children, lived on the Howard farm in peace and harmony. (A)

His father, Beverly Howard, was owned by Bill Anderson, who kept a saloon on the river front. (A)

Beverly was "hired out" in the house of Bill Anderson. He was allowed to go to the Howard farm every Saturday night to visit with his wife and children. This visit was always looked forward to with great joy, as they were devoted to the father. (A)

The Howard family was sold only once, being owned first by Dr. Page in Henry County, Kentucky. The family was not separated; the entire family was bought and kept together until slavery was abolished. (A)

Mr. Howard seems to be a very kind old man, lives in the home for aged colored people (The Alpha Home). (B)

He has no relatives, except a brother. He seems well satisfied living in the home. (B)

Submitted January 10, 1938
Indianapolis, Indiana

By: ANNA PRITCHETT
        Field Writer

Ref. (A) Mr. Matthew Hume, a former slave

Mr. Hume had many interesting experiences to tell concerning the part slavery had played in his family. On the whole they were fortunate in having a good master who would not keep an overseer who whipped his "blacks".

His father, Luke Hume, lived in Trimble County Kentucky and was allowed to raise for himself one acre of tobacco, one acre of corn, garden stuff, chickens and have the milk and butter from one cow. He was advised to save his money by the overseer, but always drank it up. On this plantation all the slaves were free from Saturday noon until Monday morning and on Christmas and the Fourth of July. A majority of them would go to Bedford or Milton and drink, gamble and fight. On the neighboring farm the slaves were treated cruelly. Mr. Hume had a brother-in-law, Steve Lewis, who carried marks on his back. For years he had a sore that would not heal where his master had struck him with a blacksnake whip.

Three good overseers were Jake Mack and Mr. Crafton, Mr. Daniel Payne was the owner who asked his people to report any mistreatment to him. He expected obedience however.

When Mr. Hume was a small boy he was placed in the fields to hoe. He also wated a new implement. He was so small he was unable to keep near enough to the men and boys to hear what they were talking about, he remembered bringing up the rear one day, when he saw a large rock he carefully covered it with dirt, then came down hard on it breaking his hoe. He missed a whipping and received a new tool to replace the old one, after this he could keep near enough to hear what the other workers were talking about.

Another of his duties was to go for the cattle, he had to walk around the road about a mile, but was permitted to come back through the fields about a quarter of a mile. One afternoon his mistress told him to bring a load of wood when he came in. In the summer it was the custom to have the children carry the wood from the fields. When he came up he saw his mistress was angry this peeved him, so that he stalked into the hall and slammed his wood into the box. About this time his mistress shoved him into a small closet and locked the door. He made such a howl that he brought his mother and father to the rescue and was soon released from his prison.

As soon as the children were old enough they were placed in the fields to prepare the ground for setting tobacco plants. This was a very complicated procedure. The ground was made into hills, each requiring about four feet of soil. The child had to get all the clods broken fine. Then place his foot in the center and leave his track. The plants were to be set out in the center and woe to the youngster who had failed to pulverize his hill. After one plowing the tobacco was hand tended. It was long green and divided into two grades. It was pressed by being placed in large hogsheads and weighted down. One one occasion they were told their tobacco was so eaten up that the worms were sitting on the fence waiting for the leaves to grow but nevertheless in some manner his master hid the defects and received the best price paid in the community.

The mistress on a neighboring plantation was a devout Catholic, and had all the children come each Sunday after-noon to study the catechism and repeat the Lord's Prayer. She was not very successful in training them in the Catholic faith as when they grew up most of them were either Baptists or Methodists. Mr. Hume said she did a lot of good in leading them to Christ but he did not learn much of the catechism as he only attended for the treat. After the service they always had candy or a cup of sugar.

On the Preston place there was a big strapping negro of eighteen whom the overseer attempted to whip receiving the worst of it. He then went to Mr. Hume's owner and asked for help but was told he would have to seek elsewhere for help. Finally some one was found to assist. Smith was tied to a tree and severely beaten, then they were afraid to untie him, when the overseer finally ventured up and loosened the ropes, Smith kicked him as hard as he could and ran to the Payne estate refusing to return. He was a good helper here where he received kind treatment.

A bad overseer was discharged once by Mr. Payne because of his cruelty to Mr. Luke Hume. The corncrib was a tiny affair where a man had to climb out one leg at a time, one morning just as Mr. Hume's father was climbing out with his feed, he was struck over the head with a large club, the next morning he broke the scoop off an iron shovel and fastened the iron handle to his body. This time he swung himself from the door of the crib and seeing the overseer hiding to strik him he threw his bar, which made a wound on the man's head which did not knock him out. As soon as Mr. Payne heard of the disturbance the overseer was discharged and Mr. Mack placed in charge of the slaves.

One way of exacting obedience was to threaten to send offenders South to work in the fields. The slaves around Lexington, Kentucky, came out ahead on one occasion. The collector was Shrader. He had the slaves handcuffed to a large log chain and forced on a flat boat. There were so many that the boat was grounded, so some of the slaves were released to push the boat off. Among the "blacks" was one who could read and write. Before Shrader could cabin them up again, he was seized and chained, taken to below Memphis Tennessee and forced to work in the cotton fields until he was able to get word from Richmond identifying him. In the meantime the educated negro issued freedom papers to his companions. Many of them came back to Lexington, Kentucky where they were employed.

Mr. Hume though the Emancipation Proclamation was the greatest work that Abraham Lincoln ever did. The colored people on his plant ation did not learn of it until the following August. Then Mr. Payne and his sons offered to let them live on their ground with conditions similar to our renting system, giving a share of the crop. They remained here until Jan. 1, 1865 when they crossed the Ohio at Madison. They had a cow which had been given them before the Emancipation Proclamation was issued but this was taken away from them. So they came to Ind. homeless, friendless and penniless.

Mr. Hume and his aged wife have been married 62 years and resided in the same community for 55 years where they are highly respected by all their neighbors.

He could not understand the attitude of his race who preferred to remain in slavery receiving only food and shelter, rather than to be free citizens where they could have the right to develop their individualism.(A)

EX-SLAVE OF ALLEN COUNTY

References: A. Ft. Wayne News Sentinel November 21, 1931
            B. Personal interview

Mrs. Henrietta Jackson, Fort Wayne resident, is distinguished for two reaons; she is a centennarian and an ex-slave. Residing ~~for~~ with her daughter, Mrs. Jackson is very active and helps her daughter, who operates a restaurant, do some of the lighter work. At the time I called, an August afternoon of over 90 degrees temperature, Mrs. Jackson was busy sweeping the floor. A little, rather stooped, shrunken body, Mrs. Jackson gets around slowly but without the aid of a cane or support of any kind. She wears a long dark cotton dress with a bandana on her head with is now quite gray. Her skin is walnut brown her eyes peering brightly through the wrinkles. She is intelligent, alert, cordial, very much interested in all that goes on about her.

Just how old Mrs. Jackson is, she herself doesn't know, but she thinks she is about 105 years old. She looks much younger. Her youngest child is 73 and she had nine, two of whom were twins. Born a slave in Virginia, record of her birth was kept by the master. She cannot remember her father as he was soon sold after Mrs. Jackson's death. When still a child she was taken from her mother and sold. She remembers the auction block and that she brought a good price as she was strong and healthy. Her new master, Tom Robinson, treated her well and never beat her. At first she was a plough hand, working in the cotton fields, but then she was taken into the house to be a maid. While there

the Civil War broke out . Mrs. Jackson remembers the excitement and
the coming and going. Gradually the family lost its wealth, the home
was broken up. everything was destroyed by the armies. Then came freedom for the slaves. But Mrs. Jackson stayed on with the master for a-
while. After leaving she went to Alabama where she obtained work in a
laundry "ironing white folks' collars and cuffs." Then she got married
and in 1917 she came to live with her daughter in Fort Wayne. Her
husband, Levy Jackson, has been dead 50 years. Of her children, only
two are left. Mrs. Jackson is sometimes very lonesome for her old
home in "Alabamy", where her friends lived, but for the most part,
she is happy and contented.

Federal Writers' Project
 of the W. P. A.
 District #6
 Marion County
 File #50-A

Page #1
Topic #240
Anna Pritchett

113

Folklore

Reference

     (A) Mrs. Lizzie Johnson, 705 North Senate avenue, Apt. 1.

     (B) Anna Pritchett, Federal Writer, 1200 Kentucky avenue.

Mrs. Johnson's father, Arthur Locklear, was born in Wilmington, N.C. in 1822. He lived in the South and endured many hardships until 1852. He was very fortunate in having a white man befriend him in many ways. This man taught him to read and write. Many nights after a hard days work, he would lie on the floor in front of the fireplace, trying to study by the light from the blazing wood, so he might improve his reading and writing. (A)

He married very young, and as his family increased, he became ambitious for them. Knowing their future would be very dark if they remained South. (A)

He then started a movement to come north. There were about twenty-six or twenty-eight men and women, who had the same thoughts about their children, banded together, and in 1852 they started for somewhere, North. (A)

The people selected, had to be loyal to the cause of their children's future lives, morally clean, truthful, and hard-working. (A)

Some had oxen, some had carts. They pooled all of their scant belongings, and started on their long hard journey. (A)

The women and children rode in the ox-carts, the men walked. They would travel a few days, then stop on the roadside to rest. The women would wash their few clothes, cook enough food to last a few days more, then they would start out again. They were six weeks making the trip. (A)

Some settled in Madison, Indiana. Two brothers and their families went on to Ohio, and the rest came to Indianapolis. (A)

John Scott, one of their number was a hod carrier. He earned $2.50 a day, knowing that would not accumulate fast enough, he was strong and thrifty. After he had worked hard all day, he would spend his evenings putting new bottoms in chairs, and knitting gloves for anyone who wanted that kind of work. In the summer he made a garden, sold his vegetables. He worked very hard, day and night, and was able to save some money. (A)

He could not read or write, but he taught his children the value of truthfulness, cleanliness of mind and body, loyality, and thrift. The father and his sons all worked together and bought some ground, built a little house where the family lived many years. (A)

Before old Mr. Scott died, he had saved enough money to give each son $200.00. His bank was tin cans hidden around in his house. (A)

Will Scott, the artist, is a grandson of this John Scott. (A)

The thing these early settlers wanted most, was for their children to learn to read and write. So many of them had been caught trying to learn to write, and had had their thumbs mashed, so they would not be able to hold a pencil. (A)

Mrs. Johnson is a very interesting old woman and remembers so well the things her parents told her. She deplores the "loose living," as she calls it of this generation. (B)

She is very deliberate, but seems very sure of the story of her early life. (B)

Submitted December 9, 1937
Indianapolis, Indiana

By: ANNA PRITCHETT
Field Writer

Ex Slave Stories
District No. 5.
Vanderburgh County
Lauana Creel

JXX?10

1. 116

The Story of Betty Jones.

From an Interview with Elizabeth Jones at 429 Oak Street, Evansville, Ind.

"Yes Honey, I was a slave. I was born at Henderson, Kentucky and my mother was born there. We belonged to old Mars John Alvis. Our home was up on Alvis's Hill and a long plank walk had been built from the bank of the Ohio river to the Alvis home. We all liked the long plank walk and the big house on top of the hill was a pretty place."

Betty Jones said her master was a rich man and had made his money by raising and selling slaves. She only recalls two house servants were mulattoes. All the other slaves were black as they could be.

Betty alvis lived with her parents in a cabin near her master's home on the hill. She recalls no unkind treatment. "Our only sorrow was when a crowd of our slave friends would be sold off, then the mothers, brothers, sisters, and friends always cried a lot and we children would grieve to see the grief of our parents."

The mother of Betty was a slave of John Alvis and married a slave of her master. The family lived at the slave quarters and were never parted. "Mother kept us all together until we got set free after the war." declares Betty. Many of the alvis negroes decided to make their homes at Henderson Kentucky. "It was a nice town and work was plentiful."

Betty alvis was brought to Evansville by her parents. The climate did not agree with the mother so she went to Princeton, Kentucky to live with her married daughter and died there.

Betty Alvis married John R. Jones, a native of Tennessee, a former slave of John Jones, a Tennessee planter. He died twelve years ago.

Betty Jones recalls when Evansville was a small town. She remembers when the street cars were mule drawn and people rode on them for pleasure. "When boats came in at Evansville, all the girls used to go down to the bank, wear-

The Story of Betty Jones.

ing pretty <u>ruffled dresses</u> and every body would wave to the boat men and
stay down at the river's edge until the boat was out of sight."   Betty
Jones remembers when the new Court House was started and how glad the men
of the city were to erect the nice building.   She recalls when the old
frame buildings used for church services were razed and new structures were
erected in which to worship God.   She does not believe in evil spirits,
ghosts nor charms as do many former slaves, but she remembers hearing her
friends express superstitions concerning black cats.   It was also a belief
that to build a new kitchen onto your old home was always followed by the
death of a member of the immediate family and if a bird flew into a window
it had come to bring a call to the far away land and some member of the
family would die.

Betty Jones was not scared when the recent flood came to within a block
of her door.   She had lived through a flood while living at Lawrence Station
at Marion County, Indiana.   "We was all marooned in our homes for two weeks
and all the food we had was brought to our door by boats.   White river was
flooded then and our home was in the White River Flats."   "What God wills
must happen to us, and we do not save ourselves by trying to run away.   Just
as well stay and face it as to try to get away."

The old negro woman is cared for by her unmarried daughter since her
husband's death .   The old woman is lonely and was happy to recieve a caller.
She is alone much of the time as her daughter is compelled to do house work
to provide for her mother and herself.   "Of course I'm a Christian," said
the aged negress.   "I'm a religious woman and hope to meet my friends in
Heaven."   "I would like to go back to Henderson, Kentucky once more , for
I have not been there for more than twenty years.   I'd live to walk the old
plank walk again up to Mr. Alvis' home but I(m afraid I'll never get to go.
costs too much.
So desire remains with the aged and memories remain to comfort the feeble.

'20148

Federal Writers' Project
  of the W. P. A.
  District #6
Marion County
File #54-A

Page #1
Topic #240
Anna Pritchett

Folklore

References

    (A) Nathan Jones -Ex-slave- 409 Blake Street.

    (B) Anna Pritchett -Federal Writer- 1200 Kentucky Avenue.

Nathan Jones was born in Gibson County, Tennessee in 1858, the son of Caroline Powell, one of Parker Crimm's slaves. (A)

Master Crimm was very abusive and cruel to his slaves. He would beat them for any little offense. He took pleasure in taking little children from their mothers and selling them, sending them as far away as possible. (A)

Nathan's stepfather, Willis Jones, was a very strong man, a very good worker, and knew just enough to be resentful of his master's cruel treatment, decided to run away, living in the woods for days. His master sent out searchers for him, who always came in without him. The day of the sale, Willis made his appearance and was the first slave to be put on the block. (A)

His new master, a Mr. Jones of Tipton, Tennessee, was very kind to him. He said it was a real pleasure to work for Mr. Jones, as he had such a kind heart and respected his slaves. (A)

Nathan remembers seeing slaves, both men and women, with their hands and feet staked to the ground, their faces down, giving them no chance to resist the overseers, whipped with cow hides until the blood gushed from their backs. "A very cruel way to treat human beings." (A)

Nathan married very young, worked very hard, started buying a small orchard, but was "figgered" out of it, and lost all he had put into it. He then went to Missouri, stayed there until the death of his wife. He then came to Indiana, bringing his six children with him. (A)

Forty-five years ago he married the second time; to that union were four children. He is very proud of his ten children and one stepchild. (A)

His children have all been very helpful to him until times "got bad" with them, and could barely exist themselves. (A)

Mr. and Mrs. Jones room with a family by the name of James; they have a comfortable, clean room and are content. (B)

They are both members of the Free Will Baptist Church; get the old age pension, and "do very well." (B)

Submitted December 15, 1937
Indianapolis, Indiana

By: ANNA PRITCHETT
     Field Writer

Albert Strope, Field Worker
Federal Writers' Project
St. Joseph County - District # 1
Mishawaka, Indiana

ADELINE ROSE LENNOX - EX-SLAVE

BIBLIOGRAPHY

A - Adeline Rose Lennox - Ex-Slave
    1400 South Sixth Street
    Elkhart, Indiana

Albert Strope, Field Worker
Federal Writers' Project
St. Joseph County - District # 1
Mishawaka, Indiana

ADELINE ROSE LENNOX - EX-SLAVE

Adeline Rose Lennox was born of slave parents at Middle - sometimes known as Paris - Tennessee, October 25, 1849. She lived with her parents in slave quarters on the plantation of a Mr. Rose for whom her parents worked. These quarters were log houses, a distance from the master's mansion.

At the age of seven years, Adeline was taken from her parents to work at the home of a son of Mr. Rose who had recently been married. She remembers well being taken away, for she said she cried, but her new mistress said she was going to have a new home so she had to go with her.

At the age of fourteen years she did the work of a man in the field, driving a team, plowing, harrowing and seeding. "We all thought a great deal of Mr. Rose," said Mrs. Lennox, "for he was good to us." She said that they were well fed, having plenty of corn, peas, beans, and pork to eat, more pork then than now.

As Adeline Rose, the subject of this sketch was married to Mr. Steward, after she was given her freedom at the close of the Civil War. At this time she was living with her parents who stayed with Mr. Rose for about five years after the war. To the Steward family was born one son, Johnny. Mr. Steward died early in life, and his widow married a second time, this time one George Lennox whose name she now bears.

Johnny married young and died young, leaving her alone in the world with the exception of her daughter-in-law. After her second husband's death she remained near Middle, Tennessee, until 1924, when she removed to Elkhart to spend the remainder of her life living

Page 2
Albert Strope, Field Worker
Federal Writers' Project
St. Joseph County - District # 1
Mishawaka, Indiana

122

with her daughter-in-law, who had remarried and is now living
at 1400 South Sixth Street, Elkhart, Indiana.

In the neighborhood she is known only as "Granny." While
I was having this interview, a colored lady passed and this conversa tion followed:

"Good morning Granny, how are you this morning?"

"Only tolerable, thank you," replied Granny.

The health of Mrs. Lennox has been failing for the past three
years but she gets around quite well for a lady who will be eight-
eight years old the twenty-fifth day of this October. She gets an
old age pension of about thirteen dollars per month.

A peculiar thing about Mrs. Lennox's life is that she says
that she never knew that she was a slave until she was set free. Her
mistress then told her that she was free and could go back to her
father's home which she did rather reluctantly.

Mrs. Lennox smokes, enjoys corn bread and boiled potatoes as
food, but does not enjoy automobiles as "they are too bumpy and they
gather too much air," she says. "I do not eat sweets," she remarks
"my one ambition in life is to live so that I may claim Heaven as
my home when I die."

There is a newspaper picture in the office along with an article
published by the Elkhart Truth. This is being sent to Indianapolis
today.

AD:DB
9-7-37

Monroe County
District # 11
October 4,1937

Submitted by:
Estella R.Dodson,
Bloomington,Ind.

123

INTERVIEW WITH THOMAS LEWIS,COLORED.

Reference:

(A)---------Thomas Lewis,North Summit Street,Bloomington,Ind.

"I was born in Spencer County,Kentucky,in 1857.I was born a slave.There was slavery all around on all the adjoining places.I was seven years old when I was set free.My father was killed in the Northern army.My mother,step-father and my mother's four living children came to Indiana when I was twelve years old.My grandfather was set free and given a little place of about sixteen acres.A gang of white men went to my grandmother's place and ordered the colored people out to work.The colored people had worked before for white men, on shares.When the wheat was all in and the corn laid by,the white farmers would tell the colored people to get out,and would give them nothing.The colored people did not want to work that way,and refused.This was the cause of the raids by white farmers.My mother recognized one of the men in the gang and reported him to the standing soldiers in Louisville. He was caught and made to tell who the others were until they had 360 men.All were fined and none allowed to leave until all the fines were paid.So the rich ones had to pay for the poor ones.Many of them left because all were made responsible if such an event ever occurred again.

Our family left because we did not want to work that way.I was hired out to a family for $20 a year.I was sent for.

My mother put herself under the protection of the police
until we could get away.We came in a wagon from our home to
Louisville.I was anxious to see Louisville,and thought it
was very wonderful.I wanted to stay there,but we came on
across the Ohio River on a ferry boat and stayed all night
in New Albany.Next morning the wagon returned home and we
came to Bloomington on the train.It took us from 9 o'clock
until three in the evening to get here.There were big slabs
of wood on the sides of the track to hold the rails together.
Strips of iron were bolted to the rails on the inside to
brace them apart.There were no wires at the joints of the
rails to carry electricity,as we have now,for there was no
electricity in those days.

I have lived in Bloomington ever since I came here.
I met a family named Dorsett after I came here.They came
from Jefferson County,Kentucky.Two of their daughters had
been sold before the war.After the war,when the black people
were free,the daughters heard some way that their people
were in Bloomington.It was a happy time when they met their
parents.

Once when I was a little boy,I was sitting on the
fence while my mother plowed to get the field ready to put
in wheat.The white man who owned her was plowing too.Some
Yankee soldiers on horses came along.One rode up to the fence
and when my mother came to the end of the furrow,he said to
her,"Lady,could you tell me where Jim Downs' still house is?"
My mother started to answer,but the man who owned her told

her to move on.The soldiers told him to keep quiet,or they
would make him sorry.After he went away,my mother told the
soldiers where the house was.The reason her master did not
want her to tell where the house was,was that some of his
Rebel friends were hiding there.Spies had reported them to
the Yankee soldiers.They went to the house and captured the
Rebels.

Next soldiers came walking.I had no cap.One soldier
asked me why I did not wear a cap.I said I had no cap.The
soldier said,"You tell your mistress I said to buy you a
cap or I'll come back and kill the whole family."They
bought me a cap,the first one I ever had.

The soldiers passed for three days and a half.They
were getting ready for a battle.The battle was close.We
could hear the cannon.After it was over,a white man went to
the battle field.He said that for a mile and a half one
could walk on dead men and dead horses.My mother wanted to
go and see it,but they wouldn't let her,for it was too awful.

I don't know what town we were near.The only town I
know about had only about four or five houses and a mill.I
think the name was Fairfield.That may not be the name,and
the town may not be there any more.Once they sent my mother
there in the forenoon.She saw a flash,and something hit a
big barn.The timbers flew every way,and I suppose killed
men and horses that were in the barn.There were Rebels
hidden in the barn and in the houses,and a Yankee spy had
found out where they were.They bombed the barn and surrounded

the town.No one was able to leave.The Yankees came and captured the Rebels.

I had a cousin named Jerry.Just a little while before
the barn was struck a white man asked Jerry how he would
like to be free.Jerry said that he would like it all right.
The white men took him into the barn and were going to put
him over a barrel and beat him half to death.Just as they
were about/to beat him,the bomb struck the barn and Jerry
    ready
escaped.The man who owned us said for us to say that we were
well enough off,and did not care to be free,just to avoid
beatings.There was no such thing as being good to slaves.
Many people were better than others,but a slave belonged to
his master and there was no way to get out of it.A strong
man was hard to make work.He would fight so that the white
men trying to hold him would be breathless.Then there was
nothing to do but kill him.If a slave resisted,and his master
killed him,it was the same as self-defense today.If a cruel
master whipped a slave to death,it put the fear into the
other slaves.The brother of the man who owned my mother had
many black people.He was too mean to live,but he made it.
Once he was threshing wheat with a 'ground-hog' threshing
machine,run by horse power.He called to a woman slave.She
did not hear him because of the noise of the machine,and did
not answer.He leaped off the machine to whip her.He caught
his foot in some cogs and injured it so that it had to be
taken off.

They tell me that today there is a place where there

is a high fence.If someone gets near,he can hear the cries
of the spirits of black people who were beaten to death.It
is kept secret so that people won't find it out.Such palces
are always fenced to keep them secret.Once a man was out
with a friend,hunting.The dog chased something back of a
high fence.One man started to go in.The other said,"What
are you going to do?" The other one said,"I want to see what
the dog chased back in there."His friend told him,"You'd
better stay out of there.That place is hanted by spirits of
black people who were beaten to death." "

XDOOOGXXXXXXDDDGDXX

-30-

TITLES IN THE
SLAVE NARRATIVES SERIES
FROM APPLEWOOD BOOKS

ALABAMA SLAVE NARRATIVES
ISBN 1-55709-010-6 • $14.95
Paperback • 7-1/2" x 9-1/4" • 168 pp

ARKANSAS SLAVE NARRATIVES
ISBN 1-55709-011-4 • $14.95
Paperback • 7-1/2" x 9-1/4" • 172 pp

FLORIDA SLAVE NARRATIVES
ISBN 1-55709-012-2 • $14.95
Paperback • 7-1/2" x 9-1/4" • 168 pp

GEORGIA SLAVE NARRATIVES
ISBN 1-55709-013-0 • $14.95
Paperback • 7-1/2" x 9-1/4" • 172 pp

INDIANA SLAVE NARRATIVES
ISBN 1-55709-014-9 • $14.95
Paperback • 7-1/2" x 9-1/4" • 140 pp

KENTUCKY SLAVE NARRATIVES
ISBN 1-55709-016-5 • $14.95
Paperback • 7-1/2" x 9-1/4" • 136 pp

MARYLAND SLAVE NARRATIVES
ISBN 1-55709-017-3 • $14.95
Paperback • 7-1/2" x 9-1/4" • 88 pp

MISSISSIPPI SLAVE NARRATIVES
ISBN 1-55709-018-1 • $14.95
Paperback • 7-1/2" x 9-1/4" • 184 pp

MISSOURI SLAVE NARRATIVES
ISBN 1-55709-019-X • $14.95
Paperback • 7-1/2" x 9-1/4" • 172 pp

NORTH CAROLINA SLAVE NARRATIVES
ISBN 1-55709-020-3 • $14.95
Paperback • 7-1/2" x 9-1/4" • 168 pp

OHIO SLAVE NARRATIVES
ISBN 1-55709-021-1 • $14.95
Paperback • 7-1/2" x 9-1/4" • 128 pp

OKLAHOMA SLAVE NARRATIVES
ISBN 1-55709-022-X • $14.95
Paperback • 7-1/2" x 9-1/4" • 172 pp

SOUTH CAROLINA SLAVE NARRATIVES
1-55709-023-8 • $14.95
Paperback • 7-1/2" x 9-1/4" • 172 pp

TENNESSEE SLAVE NARRATIVES
ISBN 1-55709-024-6 • $14.95
Paperback • 7-1/2" x 9-1/4" • 92 pp

VIRGINIA SLAVE NARRATIVES
ISBN 1-55709-025-4 • $14.95
Paperback • 7-1/2" x 9-1/4" • 68 pp

* * * * * * * * * * * * * * *

IN THEIR VOICES: SLAVE NARRATIVES
A companion CD of original recordings
made by the Federal Writers' Project.
Former slaves from many states tell
stories, sing long-remembered songs,
and recall the era of American slavery.
This invaluable treasure trove of oral
history, through the power of voices of
those now gone, brings back to life the
people who lived in slavery.
ISBN 1-55709-026-2 • $19.95
Audio CD

* * * * * * * * * * * * * * *

TO ORDER, CALL 800-277-5312 OR
VISIT US ON THE WEB AT WWW.AWB.COM

Printed in the United States
90968LV00004B/14/A

9 781557 090140